KYRIAKIS'S
INNOCENT
MISTRESS

BY
DIANA HAMILTON

First published in Great Britain 2009
Harlequin Mills & Boon Limited,
Eton House, 18-24 Paradise Road, Richmond, Surrey TW9 1SR

© Diana Hamilton 2009

ISBN: 978 0 263 87427 3

Set in Times Roman 10½ on 12¾ pt
01-0909-41447

Printed and bound in Spain
by Litografia Rosés, S.A., Barcelona

KYRIAKIS'S
INNOCENT
MISTRESS

PROLOGUE

DIMITRI KYRIAKIS stared fixedly at his father's home and told himself he wasn't overawed. No way. The villa—what he could see of it at the end of the straight tree-bordered drive—was immense: a gleaming white monument to wealth and power. No way could he walk up that driveway without knowledge of the correct sequence of numbers needed to activate the high-tech mechanism that would open the massive wrought-iron gates. And to attempt to climb them would without doubt bring security guards running.

But he'd find a way. He had to. For his mother's sake, he had to.

She was owed.

He was fourteen years old. A man. Or almost. And he'd come to collect. No power on earth could keep him from what he had to do.

Straightening his bony shoulders, he set off, scouting the high perimeter wall of the estate, the hot Greek sun burning through the cheap white fabric of his best shirt. If his mother knew what he was doing she'd throw a fit. Or several.

He tried to smile at the mental image of the gentle, frail Eleni Kyriakis losing it, but the lump in his throat rose like a spike of hot lava and pushed any attempt out of existence.

Late last night she'd told him. Returning from his after-school stint dogsbodying in the sweltering kitchens of one of Athens' most prestigious hotels—owned as he now knew by his father—to the mean, claustrophobic rooms they rented in a narrow back street, he'd found his mother bent over a pile of ironing. It was part of the one-woman laundry service she'd instigated several years before, to augment the money she earned from her daily cleaning work.

She had pushed a strand of greying hair from her forehead, and her smile had been as gently welcoming as ever, giving no clue to what was to come.

'Sit with me, my son. I have something to tell you.' She sighed softly. 'Many times you've asked who your father is, and many times I've answered that I'd tell you all about him when you were older, when maturity has brought the wisdom to see things clearly without the fog of childish emotions. But circumstances have changed.'

Her eyes had glittered with rare tears and he'd known then that something was wrong. Very wrong.

He could still feel echoes of the stomach-looping, throat-clogging sensation that had weakened his bones as she'd told him that she'd been undergoing tests. There was something wrong with her heart. It could fail her at any moment. She'd smiled then, bravely, and it was a smile he'd remember for the rest of his life.

She had taken his hands. 'But what do they know? I'm tough. I'll prove them wrong—you'll see! But just in case they're right I must tell you about your father. He was so handsome, so magnetic, and I loved him very much.'

It had been then, as she'd given him the identity of the man who had sired him, that he'd seen his beloved mother with fresh eyes. As he'd taken in the lines of exhaustion on her once beautiful face, her sunken cheeks and the tell-tale blue of her lips, he'd known exactly what he had to do.

With the determined tightening of his young jaw that was to become habitual, he began to climb the wall, muscles straining as he sought foot and hand-holds, his tension released as he swung over the top and dropped silently onto the long grass.

Beyond the belt of trees, the seeding grasses, he could see the sweep of an immaculately manicured and watered lawn—could smell, from somewhere, the evocative scent of summer-flowering jasmine, and could hear distant voices. A male, clipped and harsh, a petulant female whine.

Emerging into the full, relentless beat of the sun, Dimitri saw them. The man wearing a cream linen suit was his father. His photograph was splashed across the financial pages often enough to be instantly recognisable. The woman—young, supple—was dressed in something that floated around her body with every shift of the breeze, with every movement. She was carrying a parasol, her blonde head turned slightly away from his father. He could see the icy glint of diamonds hanging from her ears. The amount the gems must cost would have meant his mother wouldn't have had to work herself half to death for at least a couple of years.

So this had to be the second wife his mother had spoken of.

Resolve spurred him towards them, his long, gangling legs automatically taking him out into the open, where he could be seen. This wretched man, already married for the first time, with a young son, had seduced a servant in his employ and instantly dismissed her when she'd told him she was pregnant.

With *him*!

For that he would be made to pay!

He'd been seen; his intrusion had registered. Every nerve in Dimitri's skinny body stretched and his mouth went dry. But his chin came up as the man who was his father walked towards him, leaving the woman who was his wife standing.

'Who are you and what do you want?' The voice carried the harshness of the despot he was, secure in his kingdom, the wealthy owner of cruise liners and swanky hotels. One hand, Dimitri noted, went to an inner jacket pocket. Did he carry a gun? he conjectured wildly. Did he mean to shoot the shabby peasant and claim self-defence? Or was he about to use some device to summon his security officers, have him tossed back over the wall with as much ceremony as the disposal of a bundle of unspeakable rubbish?

Refusing to let his tautened nerves get the better of him, he spoke, deploring the wretched high-pitched squeak his breaking voice sometimes embarrassed him with. 'I'm Dimitri Kyriakis, son of Eleni. Your son.'

Silence, thickening in the heat of the sun. His father's hand slid back to his side. Empty.

A broad, stocky figure, black-suited, approached along a path that snaked from the villa. The woman began to move towards them. His father motioned them both back with an impatient arm movement. 'An easy claim to make! And even easier to dismiss. What do you want with me?'

The handsome features were marred by what was doubtless a perpetual sneer. Dimitri reddened. He took insults from no one, but he had no pride where his mother's wellbeing was concerned. She had worked her guts out to provide for them both, gone without food sometimes so that her son shouldn't go hungry. Never complained.

He squared his bony shoulders. He was almost as tall as the older man. He willed his voice to remain steady. 'You are Andreas Papadiamantis. Everyone knows how rich and powerful you are—all those fancy hotels and cruise liners. You have everything; my mother has nothing. Fifteen years ago Eleni Kyriakis worked here for you, as a domestic servant. You told her your marriage was finished. You seduced her. She was beautiful then and she was in love with you.' His heart leaped when he saw the unmistakable flicker of recognition in his father's eyes. He remembered her—remembered what had happened! It made what he had to say, ask, so much easier. 'But she became pregnant, and when she told you you dismissed her. I guess you broke her heart.'

She hadn't said as much, but Dimitri had sensed deep sadness when she spoke of what had happened all those years ago.

He met his father's narrowed, contemptuous eyes and stated vehemently, 'She doesn't know I'm here, speaking to you. She would never ask for anything for herself. Ever. But I will. She is ill. Her heart is exhausted. She needs rest, decent food. I do what I can. At weekends and after school I work in the kitchens at one of your hotels here in Athens. It is some help, but it's not enough.' He took a deep breath. 'All I ask is that you make her a small monthly allowance. Just enough to mean she doesn't have to work to pay the rent and buy food. And only until I am able to provide for her myself. She needs to rest, to live without anxiety,' he stressed, his voice cracking.

Rumoured to be one of the wealthiest men in

Greece, Andreas Papadiamantis wouldn't miss the outlay of a modest monthly allowance. He would probably spend more on an evening dining out with his beautiful second wife.

Refusing to let himself squirm under the relentless stare of his father's hard black eyes, Dimitri blurted, 'I want nothing for myself, and I will never ask anything else of you but this. A small allowance would mean little to you, but it would make the difference between life and an early death for my mother. Consult with her doctors if you don't believe me!'

The man who was his father smiled then. A humourless twisting of his hard, handsome mouth. And his voice was harsh. 'I don't give in to blackmail—as smarter people than you have learned to their cost. Breathe one word of this to anyone else and I will squash you and your mother as if you were beetles beneath my feet. Even if your story is true, Eleni Kyriakis knew what she was doing when she opened her legs for me. And learn this and learn it well: dog eats dog in this world, and the weak go to the wall.'

An abrupt arm movement had the security guard advancing. He had hands like hams, Dimitri noted with the small part of his mind that wasn't seething with impotent rage.

'Spiro, see this person off my property.' Not even looking at him, Andreas Papadiamantis turned and strolled back to the waiting woman, and Dimitri found himself ignominiously frogmarched to the main gates and tossed out onto the white dust of the road.

Hearing the gates clang shut, Dimitri hoisted himself back to his feet, his jaw set.

His mother had been insulted. *He* had been insulted. He hated the man who was his father. He would have his revenge. He brushed himself down and, his dark head held high, began the long trudge back to the city.

He would make his father pay for his callous insults. He would find a way.

His vow was strengthened when he discovered that there was to be no more work for him in the kitchens of his father's hotel. The loss of his meagre pay was a spiteful act on his father's part.

And the vow was set in impermeable stone when ten months later his mother died of a heart attack.

CHAPTER ONE

Dimitri Kyriakis placed the unmarked buff-coloured envelope squarely in front of him on the gleaming expanse of the otherwise empty desktop and tried not to show his distaste as he dismissed the private investigator.

With the tips of his long fingers resting on the surface of the envelope he stared out of the huge floor-to-ceiling plate glass window, seeing nothing.

He had lived for thirty-six years, a driven man, with the last twenty-two of those years spent coldly and clinically exacting vengeance on the man who was his father for the way he'd flung unforgivable insults and flatly refused to help his gentle, loving mother when she'd needed financial help as much as she'd needed oxygen and he, her son, fourteen years old, had been impotent to provide it.

Years spent working, learning, planning, taking at first tentative steps and then giant strides towards his objective: the downfall of the arrogantly powerful Andreas Papadiamantis.

Already the Kyriakis fleet of eye-wateringly luxurious cruise liners had relegated his father's dwindling fleet to scratching for the cut-price, downmarket, kiss-me-quick tourist business, and it was rumoured to be going out of business altogether.

And now his money men were working on the takeover of the last two of his father's hotels. One in Paris, the other in London. The rest had been overshadowed by the Kyriakis chain, driven out of the top end of the market and eventually sold off at a loss.

But things had changed. His father had disappeared off the radar six months ago—none of the usual mentions in the press, no sightings at his head office in Athens—and the thought of the old lion crawling into his den to lick his wounds had been oddly unsettling to Dimitri. He needed his enemy to be in the ring, fighting.

Four months into his father's apparent disappearance, his frustration and curiosity at fever-pitch, he had had the fabulous, sprawling white villa he'd only visited that once in his life watched. He had needed a clue to what was going on. To him, the spying exercise had been utterly distasteful. Ruthless in pursuit of his objectives he might be, but he was always up-front, his intentions open for anyone to see. It was the way he operated.

His dark-as-jet eyes focused at last on the panoramic view from the window: the expanse of deep blue ocean framed in the foreground by tall pines, the glimpse of the soft white sand of a rocky bay. Relaxing. Hypnotic. Or it should be. Always had been. Until today.

He came to his island retreat on average twice a year, to unwind, empty his mind. Not a fax machine, a computer, a landline in sight. But now his mind was churning with totally uncharacteristic and unwelcome indecision.

Had he done enough? Was the vendetta played out? Was it time to forget his father, let the planned takeover go? Time to allow the man who'd sired him to avoid the final humiliation? Time for Dimitri to move on, to turn his life in an entirely different direction? To turn his back on sporadic, ultra-discreet affairs, to marry, produce sons and daughters of his own—laughing, golden-limbed small people to give a gentler purpose to his life.

The black bars of his brows drew together as he finally remembered what lay beneath his fingertips. Broad shoulders tightening beneath the crisp white cotton of his custom-made shirt, he withdrew the photographs.

His father. On a terrace surrounding an immense outdoor swimming pool. Wearing his trademark cream linen suit, shades and—incongruously—a battered straw hat. The telephoto lens made him look strangely diminished. Not so the female he was touching.

He was touching the naked shoulder of arguably the most luscious blonde bimbo ever to wear a bikini. Caught in the act of turning to smile at the older man, her long silvery hair falling back from her gorgeous face, her voluptuous breasts seeming about to burst from the confines of the two scraps of dark blue fabric, she was sexual enticement on legs.

And what legs! Long, beautifully proportioned, smooth, tanned.

Abruptly he pushed the photographic images back in the envelope. He didn't need to see the others. He'd already seen enough to know that the old lion was on the hunt for a new wife to stir his ageing libido.

His father favoured blondes.

His mouth tightened to a hard, straight line as his mind swirled with the memory of that other time, that other blonde. His father's second wife. With diamonds glittering at her ears, and her floaty designer dress a whole universe away from the cheap, second-hand stuff his mother had had to wear. And his father throwing him off his property, refusing to help, refusing the modest sum that would have assuredly gone a long way to making the life of the mother of his bastard son so much easier, in all probability extending it by several precious years.

So, no, while such coldly bitter memories still existed, it wasn't over.

Andreas Papadiamantis was still unforgiven.

'A girl could get used to this, sis!'

Bonnie Wade smiled warily at her sister. Lisa

was sprawled out on a lounger, her honed, bikini-clad body still glistening from the pool, her cropped strawberry blonde hair slicked to her head.

'My two blonde babies,' her dad called them. 'One strawberry, one champagne!'

'Here—' Bonnie reached for the tube of sunblock from the marble-topped table at the side of the lounger and tossed it over. 'You don't want a dose of sunburn.'

At twenty-seven, two years Bonnie's senior, Lisa had always been her best friend. Physically and temperamentally, they couldn't be more different. Lisa was tough as old boot leather, and slim to the point of thinness, whereas Bonnie was soft as marshmallow and—to her private dismay—billowy. But they complemented each other, understood each other.

Their mum, the harrassed wife of a busy GP, had been heard to confide in her closest friend, the mother of three boisterous boys who seemed perpetually to be intent on causing grievous bodily harm to each other. 'I don't have that problem, thank heavens! Ever since little Bonnie learned to walk my two have been joined at the hip. Never a cross word!'

So, delighted as she had been to receive the seven a.m. call from the airport this morning, she still didn't understand why Lisa was here.

'I'll talk to you about it later,' the older girl had stated on the drive back to the villa. 'And before you get your knickers in a twist, the Olds are fine. It's nothing to worry about.'

Now, three hours later, she was none the wiser. As a fitness instructor to the rich and famous, Lisa usually took time off over the Christmas season, taking a three-week break and flying to where was hottest. But it seemed this year she had decided to take a week off during the summer, with a last-minute diversion to drop in on her sister on her way to Crete.

'You're sure the old guy doesn't mind me being here?' Lisa finished slapping sunblock on her legs.

'Quite sure,' Bonnie confirmed. 'When I told him I needed time off to collect you at the airport he insisted Nico drive me, and wouldn't hear of you finding a hotel.' She tweaked the starched skirts of her white uniform dress. 'So—give. Why the unexpected visit? What is there to talk about?'

Lisa hoisted herself up on one elbow. 'OK. Look, why don't you sit down—relax? I think I know how you're going to take this, but I'm not sure, so, I thought I'd stop in as I was passing and talk to you face to face.'

Bonnie shifted on the flat soles of her white canvas shoes, as near to feeling exasperation with her sister as she'd ever been. 'I'm on duty,' she pointed out. A glance at her watch confirmed it. 'Andreas is due for his exercise session in ten minutes.'

'Fair enough. Here goes… But first, how much longer are you in this job?'

'I'm supposed to sign off at the end of the week. Why?'

As a nurse, working through a highly respected agency, she specialised in remedial care. Sometimes, as now, she worked abroad, but mostly in the UK. She might be staying on longer to help this patient. Andreas Papadiamantis was a troubled man, and she'd promised to help him. But there was no time to go into that now—although the unexpected opportunity to confide in her sister later, during her off-duty hour after lunch, would be more than welcome.

'Why?' Lisa gave a wry, tight-lipped smile. 'Because Troy went to see the Olds, that's why. He says he wants you back.'

Bonnie felt her face crawl with colour. Anger, disbelief—she didn't know which. Abruptly she sat on a vacant lounger. On the eve of their wedding he'd sent his best man to tell her that he couldn't go through with it. Sorry. Would she arrange for the return of the wedding gifts? And she could keep the engagement ring.

She'd felt sorry for Brett, the bearer of the news. He'd been painfully embarrassed. Only with hindsight had she realised that she should have been feeling sorry for herself, broken-hearted. But she hadn't been broken-hearted, and Troy's supposedly magnanimous message that she could keep his ring was an insult she was still smarting over six months later.

The next morning, on what should have been her wedding day, she'd taken the ring and the unworn bridal gown to the nearest charity shop. Her parents, bless them, though alternately fussing over her and ranting at Troy's perfidy, had made all the necessary cancellations and returned the gifts, and she had just gone ahead and got on with her life as if nothing had happened.

Which, also with the clarity of hindsight, she recognised meant that Troy had done her a favour. She couldn't have been in love with him at all. He'd hurt her pride, her sense of self-worth, but, being of a cheerful, optimistic disposition she'd soon got over that.

'Apparently,' Lisa was saying, 'he gave them a real sob story. He didn't know what came over him. Burn-out, he guessed. He'd been working so hard. He'd never forgive himself for hurting you so badly, for messing up his own life, come to that. He loves you more than he thought possible, and just wants the chance to put things right. But he didn't know where you were working, how to contact you—blah-blah-blah. And you know Mum. A soppy romantic if there ever was one. She went and got all dewy-eyed and sentimental and told him where you were, working with a cancer patient. And—this is more than a guess—I know he'll be turning up any time now. As soon as he can fix time off from that supposedly mega-impressive job of his in the City. I wanted to warn you. I don't think you're the type to go all gooey when a guy gets down on his knees and begs forgiveness with crocodile tears in his eyes, but some women just might—'

'Not *this* one!' Bonnie got to her feet, a smile twitching at the corners of her expressive mouth. The nerve of the man! Though if Lisa was right, and Troy Frobisher did want them to get back together, and she *had* been head over heels in love with him, then she might be deluded enough to believe whatever he said and spend the rest of her life regretting her gullibility.

She turned to her sister. 'Thanks for the warning. We'll talk more later—after lunch. Don't worry, I won't be taken in by him—or any man, come to that. And I've got something to tell you that'll knock spots off the prospect of any sick-making visit from an ex-fiancé!'

Andreas Papadiamantis could be a charming companion when he wanted to be, and if ensuring that his surprise house-guest felt welcome and relaxed while she enjoyed the lavish hospitality of his home was his objective then he'd succeeded magnificently.

Over lunch at the polished stone-topped table in a cool, airy dining room, his gaunt, still-handsome features softened as he glanced between the sisters, smoothly switching subjects.

'Touching on your amusing description of your need for strictness with your clients, I must tell you that my nurse—your sister—is also a formidable woman,' he told Lisa. 'When I was first diagnosed and taken in for treatment I insisted on a total news blackout. I am not the powerful business force I once was, but I still have assets—the remainder of a once dominant chain of luxury hotels. If the shareholders got wind of my possible demise the value could drop like a stone.

'Bonnie was apprised of the situation when she took over my remedial care, and I tell you, although I employ a security staff, she made them look like amateurs! She was like a lioness defending her cub.' He lifted his bony shoulders in a dismissive shrug. 'I have lived with press interest for most of my life, but it has increased to intolerable proportions since my son set out to ruin me. She sent them flying— literally!' He chuckled, his black eyes dancing. 'She found one clinging to a tree that overhangs the perimeter wall on the far side of the estate. She knocked him off his perch with a handy stout stick!'

Bonnie blushed at the reminder. She'd felt dreadful afterwards, and had sent Spiro, one of the security men, out to discover if the snooper had been hurt. Thankfully there'd been no sign of the man or his camera.

'It's not something I'm proud of,' she told the grinning Lisa, and laid down her fork, her healthy appetite dwindling.

It disappeared altogether when her patient said, 'Bonnie saved my life. I truly believe that. Oh, the doctors did their part, I don't deny that, but mentally I had given up. Until Bonnie arrived and chivvied me out of it—taught me how to laugh, really laugh, for perhaps the first time in my life, to take things less seriously.' His eyes clouded. 'To take a long hard look at my life, recognise my mistakes and vow to do better. I know her agency will move her on to look after some other ailing creature when I get the final all-clear—'

'Which you have,' Bonnie put in, wanting to stop all this embarrassing stuff.

Andreas ignored her, explaining to Lisa, 'I don't want to lose her. Selfish I may be, but she has been so good for me.' His quirky grin was self-mocking. 'I even went so far as to ask her to marry me, but showing great wisdom she declined—much to an old man's disappointment!' He dabbed his mouth with his napkin. 'Now I must leave you both for my afternoon rest—as my good nurse insists.'

There was a heavy silence until the door closed behind Andreas, and then Lisa exploded, 'What was all *that* about?' She raised one arched brow. 'Did he really pop the question?'

'Come on.' Bonnie rose from the table and brushed a stray crumb from the front of the white lawn sleeveless blouse she'd teamed with an apricot-coloured cotton skirt. 'We'll find somewhere to talk.'

It was the hottest part of the day, and usually she spent her off-duty hour in the pool, but today that pleasure would have to be deferred. She was intent on unburdening herself.

For the past week she'd been itching to do just

that, but there'd been no one to confide in. Now, like
a gift from above, Lisa had arrived. She couldn't
choose a better confidante than her sister—her best
friend.

She led the way to one of the immense salons,
elaborately furnished in the high baroque style. She
privately thought it was more like a self-conscious
museum than a comfy home. But at least the air-con-
ditioning kept the interior of the villa pleasantly
cool.

'Grief!' Lisa's eyebrows arched up to her hairline.
'Who did the Disney decor?'

'The Sugar Plum Fairy?' Bonnie grinned, plonk-
ing down on a stiffly upholstered two-seater settee
and patting the space beside her.

A week ago, during her early-evening peram-
bulation of the extensive grounds with her patient,
Andreas had suggested they sit awhile in one of the
strategically placed vine-covered arbours.

Concerned that the old man who had made such
excellent progress was feeling unwell, she had been
knocked speechless when he'd come out with, 'Will
you be my wife, Bonnie? I do not ask this lightly.
You have brought optimism back into my life, given
me hope where before there was only bleak emptiness. When I was at my weakest you gave me
strength. I find I don't want to be without your life-
enhancing company, your warmth and strength. I
have been lonely for too long.'

Bonnie had gulped. The pleading darkness of the

old man's eyes had made her feel terrible. She knew that patients often got—well, crushes, for want of a better word, on their nurses, and they just as soon got over them. But Andreas was, as he'd said, so lonely. He had no friends as far as she could tell, and no family. No one to visit with bunches of grapes, no one to phone for progress reports or even send get well cards. No one. Nothing.

Too flummoxed to think of anything sensible to say, Bonnie had felt her insides shrinking until her stomach felt like a particularly tough walnut.

'It would be a marriage in name only,' Andreas assured her. 'I would make no sexual demands upon you. You would have the protection of my name—and my name still means something, even though my second son is crushing my various businesses into the ground. I have a personal fortune in a Swiss bank account—entirely separate from my business affairs. Upon our marriage it will be yours, to give you security for life. In return all I would ask of you would be your constant company and your promise to intercede with my son on my behalf.'

'I didn't know you had *any* sons!' Bonnie blurted, seizing on the outrage she felt on his behalf at his offspring's obvious uncaring neglect, in order to put off the moment when she would have to turn his marriage proposal down flat. And hadn't he said something about this second son running his business into the ground? Coming from a close-knit, loving family herself, she couldn't think of anything more chillingly vile!

'I need to be frank with you.' He took her hands. Her first instinct was to withdraw them, but the beginnings of pity took over as he confessed, 'My near brush with death has made me take stock of my life. I have too many regrets. My first marriage was arranged. We didn't love each other. At the time love wasn't important, or so I thought. There was no room in my busy life for pointless emotion. I saw emotion as a weakness. Building up my business empire was all that mattered. She—Alexandrina— died shortly after giving birth to my firstborn son, Theo.' His mouth twisted wryly. 'I honestly think she died to get away from me—and that's a heavy weight on my conscience.'

He paused, as if remembering something dark that had been buried for too long and then, his voice strengthening, continued, 'I remarried within a year. A man in his prime has certain needs, and taking a mistress entails a certain expenditure of time and effort—time that could be more profitably spent on business concerns.'

'And taking a wife *doesn't* mean spending time and effort?' asked Bonnie, appalled.

Andreas sighed deeply. 'I am telling you this to show you the man I was then. The type of man whose first unloved and unconsidered wife died to escape him, and whose second wife eventually ran off with another man. Whose firstborn son left home as soon as he hit eighteen because—as he said—I drove him too hard, expected too much, used criticism as our only mode of conversation. I never saw him again. He left my home, refused to join the business as I had planned since his birth, so I washed my hands of him. He died of a heroin overdose in Paris five years later.'

His hands tightened on hers. 'I am not proud of what I was. I have been a failure as a husband, as a father. As a human being. I see all this now, and I cannot tell you how deeply I regret it all. Regret all that I was, all that I was not. But most of all I regret that I have not seen my second son since he was fourteen years old—and that he has made himself my enemy.'

He took a deep breath. Warm darkness was closing in, the great scarlet ball of the sun sinking low on the horizon. 'That is why I would ask you, were you to agree to be my wife, to stand by my side and give me courage, to intercede with my remaining son on my behalf. I want to get to know him, make amends if I can. I dream of turning his enmity into friendship—or, if that cannot be managed, a sense of kinship. I don't want to leave this life having no one of my blood to mourn my passing.'

Bonnie felt her throat tighten, felt moisture gather in her eyes. She was so sorry for him. Poor old guy! On the face of it, he'd deserved all he got. But he was obviously truly repentant over his past deeply dreadful shortcomings. His recent near death experience had opened his eyes to his failures with shocking clarity.

Surely he deserved a second chance?

But she had to make one thing clear. Gently, she withdrew her hands from his. 'Andreas,' she began firmly, 'I'm fond of you.'

And she was. They'd hit it off from the start. She always gave her patients the best care she could, even if they were real miseries! But Andreas had been different—responding positively to all her medical demands, never once complaining. She tried her best to like all her charges, even if they were impossible, but with this old guy she hadn't had to try.

'But I can't marry you,' she said softly. 'It's immensely flattering, but in my book marriage should be more than a contract, with money changing hands. Companionship comes into it, of course, but there has to be so much more. I will promise one thing. I'll do my utmost to try and put things right between you and your son, but you must tell me how to go about it.'

'So what are you going to do?' Lisa had listened in total silence as Bonnie had recounted that conversation verbatim. 'What are you going to say to this estranged son of his? It won't be easy—but I guess you know that.'

'I'll think of something,' Bonnie replied, with a confidence she was far from feeling.

Deep down she felt this was a no-win situation. On

the one hand, the firstborn son's reaction to his father's harsh idea of parenting made it no surprise that the second-born should have followed suit. But surely that didn't excuse his apparently ruthless drive to ruin his father? A guy had to be really mean-minded to start out on *that* track, and by all accounts never give up.

Quite how she'd get through to him she had no idea. But she'd promised to do what she could, and she never went back on a promise.

CHAPTER TWO

'STAVROS!'

The sharp call cut through the searing afternoon heat, a hollow boom as the sea surged against the base of the cliffs. Suddenly feeling insecure in her resting place, a handy shady niche among the high rocks, Bonnie listened to the following spate of Greek and understood not a word, only the tone. Whoever was issuing what she suspected were orders was a guy who expected to be obeyed smartish, no questions asked. Her mouth quirked wryly. She pitied this Stavros if he was neglecting some duty or other.

Holding on to the wall of the blisteringly hot rock face, Bonnie got gingerly to her feet, stowed her water bottle, and hitched the leather strap of her canvas bag over her head and shoulder. At least there was someone around who could point her in the right direction.

Two days ago a workhorse of a ferry had deposited her and a load of what had looked like second-hand agricultural machinery on the quayside of this tiny harbour town, its pastel-coloured squat houses clustering around the deep water inlet, backed by hills thick with gnarled and ancient olive trees.

'It is not a tourist destination. Only the occasional backpacker visits,' Andreas had told her. 'From what I gather it boasts only one road, a handful of basic shops and tavernas. The lifestyle is low-key and traditional, which is why the seriously wealthy build holiday homes there, attracted by the peace and quiet. My son is one of that select number. He is there now, and my feeling is that you may find him more approachable while he is in a relaxed mood.'

If she could find him!

The mention of Dimitri Kyriakis had been rewarded with blank stares from the locals, and the widow Athena Stephanides, with whom she was lodging, courtesy of Andreas's deep purse, had merely shrugged. 'Sorry. I know of no one with that name.'

The only option she had was to head south, to the area where the super-rich built their luxurious hideaways. Complete, so Athena had divulged with much raising of eyebrows, with helipads and swimming pools of Olympian proportions. Then she'd clammed up, as if regretting that she'd said that much.

It would appear that the locals guarded the privacy of their wealthy incomers. And in all fairness Bonnie couldn't really blame them, because they obviously boosted the island economy, recruiting permanent and temporary staff from amongst the close-knit island families.

So she had no choice but to head down there and knock on doors—provided she could get past security fences and prowling guard dogs! She wasn't looking forward to it, but she had promised Andreas. Besides, she wanted to help the poor old guy, because the mistakes he'd made in the past were now deeply regretted, were troubling him, and if she could help him put them right then she was up for it.

Her idea of following the coastline and then striking inland to the southern tip of the island where the secluded villas of the mega-wealthy were located didn't seem as brilliant now as it had when she'd pored over a rudimentary map of the island after breakfast.

She might have made better progress if she had followed the long, dusty road that led over the high spine of the island. It might have been tedious in the extreme, but it wouldn't have been as hairy as this coastal shortcut was proving to be.

Far too many feet below her, deep green translucent water swelled and subsided. It made her feel giddy. Telling herself she wouldn't fall into the ocean, she wasn't that stupid, she gritted her teeth and edged forward around the outcrop, heading for what her map had told her was a small horseshoe-shaped bay. From there, as far as she could make out, an unmade track led further south, skirting the central rocky spine of the island.

Successfully negotiating the obstacle, she paused,

expelled the breath she hadn't realised she'd been
holding, then sucked in another, deeper gulp of air.
The cove below her *was* idyllic, but even more spectacular was the man walking along the waterline
carrying driftwood.

Tall, tanned, magnificently built, his sleek musculature of wide shoulders and deep chest narrowed
down to lean hips clad in shabby, ragged-hemmed
denim cut-offs.

Stavros?

His long, relaxed stride halted as he turned and
stared out to sea. He hadn't seen her, clinging to the
rocks high above. Suddenly it seemed imperative
that she get down to him. Only to ask him to point
her in the right direction for the track that would take
her to her objective, of course. Conversing, if only
briefly, with such a gorgeous hunk would be a bonus!

Grinning at her very natural female folly, she
began to scramble on, and caught her foot in a
fissure. She let out a yelp of pain, and cursed herself
roundly for not looking where she was going.

Clinging awkwardly to the rock, she bent to rub
the offending ankle, a slippery hank of long silvery
blonde hair falling over her face as it escaped the
pins that had secured it in a knot on top of her head.
A sob of frustration blocked her throat as she discovered that she couldn't put her weight on the foot.

Now how was she going to get back? Get *any-
where*? There was no public transport on the tiny
island, and even if she could hobble—or crawl!—

to the only proper road some way inland she might have to wait hours before she could thumb a lift in some passing truck back to the small fishing port where she was based.

'Stay where you are.'

Annoyance with herself, and frustration over her self-inflicted plight, had driven the stranger on the shore below right out of her mind. But now—well, he had abandoned the driftwood and was climbing up towards her, with a lithe efficiency that widened her smoky grey eyes with admiration and made her heart pump a little faster.

Close to, he was even more knee-tremblingly sensational than her first assessment had led her to believe. And as that first assessment had given him top marks plus in the eye candy category, all Bonnie could do was stare while her entire body went into melting jelly mode.

His face was as stunning as the rest of him. No pretty-boy good-looks these. Hard lines and an angular bone structure carried the stamp of the alpha adult male. Tough, darkly shadowed jawline, and silky black hair, eyes as dark as jet.

Her own eyes fell in a trembling heartbeat to a wide mouth that was a shattering mixture of the sensual and the ruthless.

Wordlessly, he was returning the shockingly intimate intentness of her visual assessment and Bonnie dropped her eyes, her face flaming as something like an electric charge skittered through her.

His bare feet were planted firmly apart on the rock as he finally spoke, his deep, only faintly accented voice sending ripples down her spine. 'You are hurt. Will you trust me to get you down from this place?'

Pulling herself together, Bonnie found her voice. 'Of course. Thank you. I'd be grateful.' She attempted a smile. It wobbled. What was wrong with her? She had both her feet firmly on the ground—metaphorically, if not physically at this precise moment—and she wasn't the air-headed type to go to pieces just because she'd happened across the most lip-smackingly gorgeous man to inhabit the planet.

She was a practical, down-to-earth qualified remedial nurse and—

Every last sensible thought was swept out of her head as the gorgeous stranger hoisted her, without apparent effort, into a fireman's lift and carried her down the steep rocks with the surefootedness of a mountain goat.

Carefully depositing her on the soft white sand, he hunkered down in front of her, long, deft fingers gently exploring her injured foot.

His touch was magic. A lock of soft black hair fell forwards over his tanned forehead. She wanted to run her fingers through it.

Stupid woman!

She was shivering all over.

Merely the entirely natural after-effects of her hairy passage down from the cliffs!

Only she hadn't felt scared. She'd felt safe—gloriously safe.

'Just a slight sprain and a tiny cut,' he pronounced, a smile playing at the corners of that devastating mouth. 'I'll take you to the house and clean the cut.'

Forcing herself out of the entirely unwelcome ditzy-schoolgirl-meets-pop-star mode, Bonnie located her best no-nonsense voice and used it. 'You've been very kind already, but—Stavros, is it?—I don't want to put you to any more trouble on my account. I'm sure that if I just rest a while I'll be fine to go on.'

Dimitri Kyriakis didn't correct her.

She must have heard him calling to his manservant/minder, to remind him to drive down to the port to collect the incoming mail that had been waiting for two days since the weekly ferry had docked.

The longer his father's blonde, gold-digging bimbo remained in ignorance of his true identity the better.

His father had taste, though, he conceded grimly. The bimbo was even more enticingly sexy in the flesh than she'd appeared in the photograph. All that long, silky pale blonde hair, falling in a tousled touchable mass to well below her shoulders.

Pretty shoulders, sleek of skin, warm with tan, partially concealed by the turquoise-blue halter top that lovingly cradled truly superb full and shapely breasts. Her cropped top left her tanned midriff naked and tempting above a pair of skimpy shorts. And those legs—

'It will be no trouble,' Dimitri contradicted her truthfully. 'It would be my pleasure to help you.'

Help you to unburden yourself, to tell me exactly what a woman with her eyes on the opportunity to marry an old man for his money is doing scrambling around on an island hardly anyone has heard about, out of her preferred milieu of fancy restaurants, swish hotels and designer boutiques.

Unless, of course, the old man was with her. It seemed unlikely. And did she know that Andreas Papadiamantis was facing a vastly reduced financial status? He guessed not.

She would run like a rabbit if he told her. There was only one reason a beautiful young woman would shack up with an old man, he decided, with the cynicism born of long experience of the female sex. Inform her of the non-existence of the bottomless pit of money and she'd take to her toes.

Yet there was a more entertaining way of depriving his enemy of his bed companion, he thought, staring into a pair of beguiling smoke-grey eyes.

He had never had any trouble in attracting the female sex. Quite the opposite. But he never knew whether his personality was the attraction or his massive wealth.

The latter, he suspected.

It cut both ways. On the few occasions when he'd

taken a mistress, he had made it plain that he didn't do long-term.

So what was new? Earlier he'd played with the idea of settling down, creating a family. Seeing the photograph of this blonde had had the idea taking a nosedive. Meeting the blonde in the flesh had killed it stone-dead. For a while. The fates had delivered another chance to take his revenge for what his father had done all those long years ago right into his lap.

Never one to lose an opportunity, Dimitri swept the delectable gift from the fates up into his arms. His smile as she wound her arms around his neck with a gaspy little sigh was grim. And satisfied.

He *had* her!

CHAPTER THREE

DIMITRI deposited her on a padded cane chair in the shadiest part of the vine-covered, granite-paved terrace. His heavy-lidded, lash-veiled eyes moved with lazy assessment over her body, taking in the tempting swell of her full breasts, tiny waist and voluptuous hips, resting finally on her wide, generous mouth.

Mistress material.

Quite definitely.

Yet as far as he knew—and he had tracked his enemy through the years with the dedication of a jungle cat stalking its prey—his father didn't take high-maintenance mistresses. He'd come to know how the older man's mind worked.

Too great an expenditure of time, effort and money was involved in establishing a mistress.

He would regard it as an unnecessary indulgence.

A wife was different. A wife could be safely ignored, treated as part of the furniture until he had need of her. His extra-marital adventures were furtive backstairs episodes, if his poor mother's sorry experience was anything to go by.

This bimbo would be angling for a wedding ring. She was no wide-eyed innocent to be dazzled simply by the attentions of her lord and master—not the way *she* looked, she wasn't!

Aware that he could be in danger of making assumptions, he mentally ran over the known facts. His father had been off the radar for several months, holed up in his luxurious villa. With this blonde?

Judging by that photograph, she had already got herself firmly embedded in his father's villa, up close and personal, and an announcement in the press that Andreas Papadiamantis was to take wife number three would appear in the very near future. It was practically a certainty.

How his enemy would be congratulating himself that he had got such a luscious creature to warm his old bones and his bed, whenever he chose to avail himself of such comforts.

Unless he, Dimitri Kyriakis, stopped it.

And that could be fun, as well as turning the screw a little tighter.

Bonnie squirmed against the cushions. She could feel a blush spreading all over her. The way this Stavros guy was looking at her was seriously unsettling.

Everywhere his hot gaze wandered it felt as if he was actually touching her. Her heartbeat quickened and fire licked her skin, a languorous warmth spreading through her, hot and heady, making her breasts feel swollen and heavy, their tips standing to attention within the confines of her halter top. This rivetingly sexy guy could so easily make her forget she was a sensible adult woman, with her head firmly screwed on.

Once bitten twice shy, she reminded herself staunchly.

Though being nibbled by *those* strong white teeth would be no hardship at all!

Struggling to find something mundane to say, to break the spiralling sexual tension, Bonnie expelled a gusty sigh of relief when he came to her aid.

'I'll make that ankle more comfortable. Wait here.' He disappeared through open, immense sliding glass doors into what she guessed to be his boss's luxury home.

Stavros's temporary absence gave Bonnie a much needed breathing space, and the opportunity to don her sensible hat again. So, OK, he was the most charismatic, sexy guy she'd ever come across. But better than that he was probably *local*, working for one of the island's wealthy incomers. The chances were he would be able to tell her where to find the elusive Dimitri Kyriakis.

True, according to Andreas, his estranged son only used his island villa occasionally. But on the upside, in a small place like this everyone knew everyone else. It was a close-knit community, with the locals making a living as best they could from the sea and the land. The local grapevine would be buzzing with the doings, the to-ing and fro-ings, of the wealthy other half.

So her smile was radiantly expectant when he reappeared, carrying what appeared to be enough medical supplies to stock a medium-sized pharmacy.

'I think you could help me,' she opened, as he knelt in front of her and began to clean the cut on her ankle with cotton wool soaked in something really soothing.

Dimitri frowned. That smile of hers would light up a room. But what gave him pause was the complete lack of artifice. In his experience gold-diggers—and that included beautiful young women who would marry an old man for his money—had artifice oozing from every pore. 'That is what I'm doing,' he stated, dabbing the cut dry and applying a plaster.

'No—I mean—yes. What I mean is—' Bonnie tried quite desperately to ignore the fluttery feeling that had taken over her insides as soon as those long, cool fingers of his had touched her skin. Tried to stop wanting to run her fingers through the thick, silky black hair that fell in such intriguing disarray over his downbent head. She wanted to touch it so much it was almost a physical pain. 'I mean—well, I'm trying to locate someone.'

'Yes?' Dimitri bound her ankle tightly, and deftly secured the bandage with a tiny pin. It seemed as if he was about to discover what his father's woman was doing on the island. 'That should support it adequately, though you'll have to rest it for a couple of days. You were saying?' he prompted coolly.

Bonnie blinked. Having this hunk kneeling at her feet took her breath away. No man, not even Troy— and she'd been on the brink of marrying *him*, for goodness' sake!—had ever had this effect on her.

Wondering where her sensible hat had got to, she pushed on. 'He's got a villa somewhere around here. He doesn't come often, but he's here now. And, oh— how silly!—you don't know who I'm talking about! His name's Dimitri Kyriakis—have you heard of him? Do you know where his place is?'

Dimitri got to his feet, straightening his lean, powerful figure to its full six feet three inches. His narrowed eyes were darkly probing, and the shock of hearing his name on his father's bimbo's lips hardened his voice. 'Why do you want to know?'

Very few people knew of his bolthole. No more than three. All of them were completely trusted, loyal employees who would die rather than disobey his orders. One of them being his manservant Stavros.

So it had to be down to his enemy. Andreas must have had his spies out, tracking him minutely even as *he* had tracked the older man through the years. It made sense. Dimitri's brain clicked into overdrive. He didn't like mysteries, and this one was solved in ten seconds flat.

He could think of at least two reasons why the old man had sent this woman to find him.

To push him over a cliff to get rid of him.

Or, and far more likely, to use every feminine wile and trick in the book to get close to him and learn of his future intentions via pillow talk.

Did the old man think he would be that indiscreet? That much of a sucker?

But it would be interesting to find out how far she was prepared to go...

Bonnie's heart was busily sinking. For a moment there Stavros had looked really intimidating. And now draining disappointment had taken her over. Was he going to be the same as the other islanders? Button-lipped when it came to giving information about the revered wealthy part-time residents on whom a large part of the island economy depended? It certainly looked like it.

And there was no way she could answer his question. The reason Andreas wanted her to contact Dimitri Kyriakis was between him and his son—private, and not to be given out to the first stranger who asked. She felt utterly hopeless, and, as that was an emotion she had never encountered before, faintly queasy.

Then everything changed.

'I will make enquiries for you.'

In receipt of the shatteringly charismatic smile that came her way, accompanied by that welcome and unexpected offer of help, Bonnie breathed, 'Thank you! I'd be so grateful!' and wondered why she sounded like a giddy schoolgirl instead of the sensible woman she knew herself to be.

Just how grateful? Dimitri wondered, marvelling at the tightening of his groin at the prospect of finding out—an instant physical reaction he hadn't experienced since he was a teenager.

He leaned forward and took her hands. And as his fingers tightened around hers and he met her huge smoky eyes he knew that finding out would be no problem for either of them.

She oozed warm, womanly willingness from the hazy eyes, the parted pink lips and the hardening swell of her bounteous breasts, confined by the thin top she was wearing. She was hot for him. He would swear to it.

He discreetly screened his dark eyes beneath thickly fringing black lashes. Play it cool—see how far she would go. If she'd taken her orders from his father to seduce him into revealing his future plans, then she would have to *work* for the privilege of sharing his bed. Providing he could keep his amazingly rampant libido in check, it would amuse him to watch her at work.

And when he submitted, as he knew he eventually would—because why would he deny himself the undoubted pleasure?—she would learn nothing from him, have only failure to report.

He knew himself to be a past master at getting what he wanted with the least effort to himself. 'Where are you staying?' he asked.

He was still holding her hands. It felt more than good. He was a total stranger, and she knew nothing about him. But he made her feel safe. Because he'd come to her rescue when she'd been floundering around on those rocks? Had promised to help her locate the whereabouts of Andreas's son? Or was there more to it than that?

'By the harbour, with Athena—the widow Stephanides,' she answered, her voice strangely thick, her mouth trembling just a little as he slid his hands until they rested beneath her elbows.

'I know her.' He helped her to stand on her uninjured foot, a supportive arm sliding around her small waist. 'It is well known that she caters for the occasional backpacker who turns up on the island. But you are no backpacker.'

A thread of humour laced his voice as the pressure of his arm brought her lush body into closer contact with his. With his free hand he brushed the silvery fall of her hair away from her face with gentle fingers. 'You are on a man-hunt, *ne*?'

Wild colour flooded Bonnie's cheeks. Her lips parted but no sound emerged. Put like that, it sounded awful—full of wicked sexual connotations. And she *felt* wicked, she thought chaotically. Her body was straining against this half-naked man, his bare torso hot and hard against her tingling breasts, his naked thighs tangling with hers.

Colour bloomed even more fiercely. Until he said prosaically, 'I'll drive you back.' And picked her up as if she were a sack of potatoes.

The temptation to kiss her had been almost overwhelming, but Dimitri had never given in to temptation in his life and wasn't about to start now. He knew how to play the long game.

A hot, dusty track led to a low stone building, formerly a barn, where his vehicles were housed, benefiting for part of the day from the thick shade of the pines.

Stavros had taken the imposing Range Rover, which left the much humbler buggy—more fitting transport for the local odd-job man she obviously took him to be, he decided, hiding a grim smile as he eased her down into the passenger seat.

'It will not be a comfortable ride,' Dimitri imparted with a flash of a gleaming white smile, starting the engine with a rattle and roar that reverberated horrendously within the stone barn. The exhaust needed fixing, he noted, accelerating out of the shade and onto the hot track that wound between rounded hillocks festooned with aromatic wild rosemary.

Not for him the landscaped, meticulously tended surrounds of the other villas, further down the coast. Nor the electronically operated ornate cast-iron gates and artificially blue swimming pools, or the small army of servants recruited from amongst the local population to make sure the pampered inhabitants didn't have to do anything so primitive as lift a finger for themselves.

When he came to the island he left all the trappings of wealth behind. All he asked for was a view of the ocean, fishing from the rocks when he felt like it, the long room with its vaulted ceiling, cool floor tiles, the immense white stone fireplace large enough to take chunky olive branches should the evening demand a fire—and his books, of course. Those he could never find time to read in what he regarded as the other part of his life.

'Smoother now,' he announced above the noise of the engine as the track joined the only proper road where it began its descent from the craggy spine of the island to the harbour. 'But only just, *ne*?' He grinned as they hit a pothole of majestic proportions.

Bonnie could only grit her teeth and hang on to the sides of the unsprung seat, reminding herself that jolting along at speed in an open buggy with the wind of their passage tossing her hair into wild knots and hurling insects into her face was better than having to hop or hobble her way back.

When they finally reached the outskirts of the tiny harbour village, her escort had to slow down to avoid crashing into an ancient estate wagon on the steep, narrow street, easing past the taverna where old men sat, apparently just watching the world go by, the single grocery store, and the pastry shop where the most delicious bread Bonnie had ever tasted could be bought. She could say, without fear of her mouth being invaded by flying insects, 'I can't thank you enough, Stavros. You've been so kind.' Which was, she thought, exactly the right tone—the tone of a normally ultra-capable woman who found herself temporarily indebted to a total stranger.

Then she remembered that she needed him to keep his promise to make enquiries as to where she could find Andreas's estranged son, and felt horribly torn between a self-protective desire never to clap eyes on this incredibly sexy man again and a regrettable, fizzing excitement that invaded and intensified every last one of her female hormones at the thought of sharing time with him.

Just as the buggy came to a welcome halt in front of the widow Stephanides's pink-painted house, she managed, 'The least I can do is offer you a cold drink before you head back. I'll have a word with Athena.'

He turned to her, keeping his eyes veiled, hiding the question. The invitation had been delivered in the prim and prissy, almost curt tone that had coloured her politely couched words of thanks. He'd expected something much more come-hither, given the vibes he'd earlier felt, coming from her in hot, sexy waves.

Two could play that game.

'Thank you, no. Can you manage?'

She only had to reach out a hand to hold on to the plastered wall that fronted the pink property. There was a narrow strip of paving before the open front door, behind which he could see the widow Stephanides emerging from the cool, darkened interior.

He didn't want an encounter with the garrulous

Athena. She'd call him by his given name, and it was too early to let the huntress know she'd found her quarry.

Bonnie recognised a brush-off when she heard one. Declining her invitation, his voice had been chillingly authoritative. He couldn't wait to see the back of her. He was already gunning the engine. Stupid to feel hurt and rejected.

Swinging her good foot to the ground, and grabbing on to the low wall for support, she heaved herself out of the buggy. She'd thanked him already. There was nothing more to be said. Pointless to remind him that he'd said he'd try to locate Dimitri Kyriakis for her.

He'd probably only made the offer to close the subject. Had no intention of following through. Like the rest of the local population, he was keeping his mouth shut.

'Wait.'

Schooling a look of mild enquiry onto her usually expressive features, Bonnie turned. His smile knocked her sideways, and her tummy cartwheeled as she met the glint of his brilliant dark eyes.

'Tell me your name.'

Insanely conscious of how shatteringly, sexily handsome he was, she struggled to appear cool and detached, to find her voice and state—flatly, she hoped—'Bonnie. Wade.'

She felt her cheeks burn with colour and her breath fly from her lungs as he returned, 'Bonnie. It suits you. Bonnie, indeed.' And he allowed sultry dark eyes to slowly caress the abundance of her lush breasts, her taut naked midriff and curvy hips, before raising a well-made hand in a farewell salute and driving away, leaving her clinging to the wall and weakly wondering why this guy—*any* guy—could make her feel so shamefully wanton and wicked.

CHAPTER FOUR

'DON'T distress yourself,' Andreas urged. 'My son guards his privacy well.' The tone of his voice hinted, just a little, at admiration, then he sighed heavily, making Bonnie feel dreadful. 'Perhaps I was too optimistic in hoping that he would be found in a relaxed holiday mood and so be more open to listen to you.'

Bonnie could imagine in graphic detail the resigned shrug of the frail man's bony shoulders, and she bit her lip as he made a huge effort to sound upbeat and tried to reassure her. 'But you have one more week to continue your search. Much can happen in that time. And whatever does happen I know you'll have done your best.'

But had she? Bonnie ended the catch-up call and slipped her mobile back into her purse. Despite the old man's sympathetic words, he hadn't been able to hide his disappointment when she'd phoned through at the end of her first week here to report utter failure.

One more week didn't sound like much—especially as she had accomplished nothing during the last seven days. And there was no way she could extend her stay here. She'd intended to take three weeks' leave, and for the last one she was due to be at her parents' home in England, to celebrate her father's sixty-fifth birthday and retirement.

She ground her teeth in frustration. She had so wanted to help the poor old guy. He was obviously deeply sorry for his past horrible behaviour regarding his sons, and, having had a stark reminder of his own mortality, was desperately anxious to at least try to put things right between him and the one son remaining to him.

Questioning Athena, she'd learned that the wealthy incomers arrived on the island either by helicopter or by one of the gleaming yachts moored in the harbour. But that information had gained her absolutely nothing. Down at the quayside, carefully casual questioning about the ownership of the various gleaming craft had elicited nothing more than vague shrugs and a rapid change of subject.

What had made her fume so impotently had been her wretched ankle. Hobbling around with the aid of the walking stick Athena had loaned her meant that progress in her quest had been impossible, given the closed-mouth policy of what seemed to be the entire local community. But now, five days after the mishap, it was better.

And she was going to do something positive.

Find Stavros, for starters.

For the past few days of relative inactivity she'd haunted the village, hoping to see him. Not a sign. Fool! Had she *really* believed he would come calling to tell her he'd done as he'd said he would and located the elusive Dimitri Kyriakis?

He'd probably forgotten all about her and his offer to help. A jaw-droppingly gorgeous guy, he would practise his pulling power on any female that crossed his path. He wouldn't be able to help himself—his ego would demand it. Then, satisfied that he could make the said female go all gooey-eyed, he would promptly forget her.

He'd made her go weak-kneed. And how. It must have shown, she decided in self-disgust.

But that had been then, and this was now. She didn't want to see him for his own sake—perish the thought! She merely wanted to remind him of his promise, and if possible make him feel bad about his failure to deliver. So bad that his conscience might prick him into actually doing something. Finding out where the guy was holed up was all she needed. Stavros could leave the knocking on doors and, if it came down to it, breaking in to her!

Slathering sunblock on her exposed skin, she dug a battered straw hat from the bottom of her suitcase, because the heat today—as usual—was fierce, and sped down the stairs. She called a farewell to Athena and hit the village street.

She knew where Stavros worked, and she had the

perfect excuse for dropping by. That day, after he'd carried her down from the rocks, she'd left her rucksack behind. She would explain that she had come to retrieve it. Not that there was anything in it that she couldn't live without, but he wouldn't know that.

And then she'd remind him of his promise. And make sure he explained why he hadn't followed through!

Swinging the buggy off the unmade track, Dimitri curled his sensual mouth with satisfaction as he moderated his speed and headed the vehicle towards the solitary figure trudging uphill.

Her glorious hair was bundled beneath an old floppy-brimmed straw hat, but the rest of her was delightfully, delectably on view.

A sleeveless white vest top clung lovingly to her beautiful breasts, and the softly rounded flare of her hips was covered by a pair of tiny ice-blue shorts that emphasised the warm tan and the enticing length of her fabulous legs.

A tide of warmth spread through his groin. No problem. He'd judged that he'd left her to stew for long enough and he'd obviously been right—because she was coming to find him!

The contents of her rucksack had revealed nothing. Sunblock, dark glasses, a water bottle and a not very detailed map of the island. He'd noticed the rucksack beside the chair she'd been using, and he hadn't passed it to her when he'd picked her up and carried her to the buggy, hoping that some clue to her business on the island, her searching for him, would come to light.

Nothing. Whatever her reasons for trying to track him down, they were locked securely inside her pretty head.

And it *was* an extremely pretty head, he approved as they drew level and he applied the brakes. Smoky eyes, shaded both by the brim of her hat and by long gold-tipped lashes, baby-smooth sun-kissed skin with a slight sprinkling of freckles across the bridge of her delectable nose, and that mouth—kissable, and how!

'Looking for me?' He was the first to break the silence, one dark brow lifted in sardonic interrogation.

How did he *do* that? Bonnie wondered, floundering. Look both so casually, sexily relaxed, in a dark, torso-hugging T-shirt and shabby cargo pants, his black hair boyishly rumpled, and yet so forcefully, chillingly arrogant at the same time?

She shifted restively, then managed, 'I left my rucksack behind the other day.'

Breathless. The result of her uphill climb, or something else? A pulse was fluttering frantically at the base of her smooth throat. She didn't look out of condition—far from it. Far more likely was the thought of what his father had persuaded her to do: get up close and very personal in order to discover his future plans where the old man's remaining business assets were concerned.

Yet that didn't fit either. The sort of woman who would hook up with an old man for what she thought she could get out of him wouldn't bat an eyelid at the prospect of a little sexual espionage!

'I was bringing it down to you,' Dimitri answered belatedly, aware that he'd been staring at her with fixed intensity and that she was looking decidedly uncomfortable, fidgeting and staring at her feet. An enigma to be solved. For the first time in his adult memory he experienced an upsurge of pure pleasurable sexual anticipation. 'Jump in.'

For a moment a tart refusal hovered on her lips. She became a mass of over-excited hormones in his vicinity. It was an affliction she had never thought would affect her and she deplored it. Then, just in time, she remembered he was probably her best bet—in fact her only hope—in her search for Andreas's son.

Swallowing heavily, Bonnie clambered into the uncomfortable passenger seat, her tummy full of wildly fluttering butterflies. It would take hardly any time for him to drive her down to the harbour village and offload her, which meant she had to get her act together—and quickly. Had to stop letting all that weird sexual magnetism get to her, driving everything sensible out of her head—even, unbelievably, the real reason she'd come looking for him.

She dragged in a deep, calming breath.

Opening her mouth to remind him of his promise to try to locate Dimitri Kyriakis, she pushed out instead, 'Where are you going?' as he executed an immaculate U-turn, pointing the buggy away from the village.

'I think we should spend a little time getting to know each other. You are on holiday, and I have time on my hands,' he answered with smooth confidence. 'Besides, we both know we have things to discuss,' he added pointedly. He was very comfortable with the fact that he knew who she was, who had sent her here to find him, and very possibly why.

He was one step ahead in the game and he intended to stay that way.

'Oh.' For the life of her, Bonnie couldn't manage anything more intelligent. She was streetwise enough to know that one didn't allow oneself to be picked up and whisked away, destination unknown, by a virtual stranger—even if he *was* as compellingly beautiful as a modern-day Greek god—but she hadn't been able to control an electrifying spike of unstoppable excitement when he'd talked about getting to know each other, at the wicked possibilities that threw up!

Never before in the whole of her life had she been moved to say of herself that she didn't have the sense she'd been born with!

On the other hand he was quite right. They *did* have things to discuss. Like the whereabouts of the elusive Dimitri Kyriakis, and how she might feasibly get in touch with him.

Satisfied that her fabled common sense hadn't completely deserted her, Bonnie relaxed enough to stretch her legs out into the deep well of the buggy. She encountered her rucksack and what appeared to be a cool box, and enquired calmly, 'So where are we heading?' wondering if it was too much to hope that their destination was the Kyriakis home.

For long moments he didn't respond. Frowning a little, she glanced at him—at his bold profile, the masculine jut of a cheekbone, the uncompromising set of his mouth and hard, blue-shadowed jawline.

Without taking his eyes off the way ahead, Dimitri swung the buggy off the road, onto an unmade track that snaked around the hillside, and informed her carelessly, 'Somewhere secluded. That will suit you?'

Dimitri had to force himself not to laugh. If his suspicions were right, and she was here with the intention of using her considerable assets to seduce her aged lover's son into revealing his future business plans, then just how far would she be prepared to go to 'persuade' him? She believed him to be a local odd-job man, going by the name of Stavros. How would she get him to tell her where the old man's son could be found?

The possibilities were endlessly amusing.

Bonnie knotted her fingers together in her lap and swallowed. Hard. What did he mean by that? Why would somewhere secluded suit her?

In her line of work she had learned how to handle

all types of patients in all types of moods and situations. But handle him?

She shivered.

'All I want—' Bonnie squawked and clutched her stomach as the buggy bounced over a rock. She decided to cut to the chase. 'All I want is to know whether or not you've found this Kyriakis guy.'

She'd have to do better than that. A whole lot better! Dimitri levelled her a glance from brilliant black eyes and applied the brakes. 'Do you like it?'

Disorientated by his obvious reluctance to answer her question—which probably meant he hadn't even bothered to try and make enquiries, and had dragged her into the back of beyond for no good reason— she snapped, 'Like what?'

She earned herself a lazy smile, the sort that was guaranteed to tie her stomach in knots.

'Look.'

Lean fingers tilted her chin so that she was looking out over the side of the buggy. Despite herself, a gasp of astonishment emerged from Bonnie's parted lips. They were on a natural plateau, surrounded on three sides by crumpled hills, looking out through a grove of twisted olive trees to the deep blue of the sea.

'There is a path of sorts down through the trees to the beach, where there is soft white sand. And total peace. No one comes here. It is one of my favourite places on the island.'

His hand dropped. Her skin burned where those

long, inescapable fingers had been. 'It's lovely,' she managed, and found herself unable to raise an objection when he spoke again.

'The man you want to find comes to the island to escape the relentless pressures of his normal life for a little while. Yes? Perhaps he won't want to be disturbed? Though maybe if he knew a beautiful woman wanted to speak with him he would set his reluctance aside?'

The look he dealt her was explicit, roving from her breasts to the honey-toned smoothness of her thighs revealed by the shorts she'd now decided were too short. And yet—

She needed to ignore the spiralling twist of electrifying excitement that was sending her pulses racing, Bonnie told herself sharply, trying amidst the turmoil to focus on what he was saying.

'We'll eat, drink a little, relax, and then we will discuss.'

He had actually called her beautiful! And her head was still reeling from that uninvited compliment. Mourning the loss of her normal calm and sensible take on life, she could find nothing rational to say as he took hold of the cool box in one hand and her hand in the other and led her between the trees. Twice she stumbled on the rough path, because her head was too busy warring with the sensations invading her body, transmitted by the touch of his lean, cool hand, to give any thought to where she was putting her feet.

The first time she stumbled he released her hand and snaked his arm around her waist, steadying her. The second time he pulled her even closer to his magnificent body, making heat curl insidiously in the pit of her tummy, weakening her to such an extent that she had to grit her teeth and make herself deny the urge to sag against him, melt into him.

'We'll eat in the shade,' he announced, as the white shore appeared before them and the sea glittered beneath the sun like diamonds.

An ancient, long-unpruned olive tree cast a hazy shade, and Bonnie flopped to the soft ground beneath it gratefully—because if she'd been held so closely to him for a moment longer goodness only knew what sort of fool she might have made of herself.

He should come with a government health warning, she decided wryly. She watched, unable to drag her eyes away, the play of muscles in his strong, tanned forearms as he unpacked the cool box, wondering if any woman on the planet would be safe when in his company.

Or was he safe from herself? she elaborated fairly. Because he wasn't making passes. When he'd touched her it had only been to save her from her own clumsiness.

She only had herself to blame, she decided sensibly as he handed her a platter of feta, tiny tomatoes and olives. Around Stavros she couldn't control her sexuality. Fact. Such lack of control had never happened to her before. Fact.

And she deplored it. It simply wasn't in her character. She should never have agreed to let him bring her here. She should have insisted he drive her back to the village or, failing that, made him leave her at the side of the road to make her own way back.

But then she remembered.

Andreas's son. She was sure Stavros could help her. The way he'd talked about the Greek tycoon escaping to his island retreat to escape the pressures of his busy life suggested that he knew the guy. She just had to convince him to tell her where she could *find* Dimitri Kyriakis.

Feeling more like herself, more in control of the situation, Bonnie concentrated on the food—it really was delicious—and carefully avoided looking at Stavros. She would start the discussion he had mentioned just as soon as she had cleared her plate.

But the moment she had done so she found a glass of ice-cold sparkling wine placed in her hand. Their fingers brushed as she took it, and her heart beat a crazy tattoo as heat suffused her entire body. To quell it, she tilted the glass and dispensed with the contents in two huge gulps.

Stavros said, his voice warm and slow, 'You are hot, *pethi mou*.'

Horribly aware of the direction of his eyes, she knew the upper part of her chest, which the V neck of her sleeveless vest top left bare, was beaded with perspiration. Lower down the soft fabric was clinging to her lush curves. Instinctively dipping her head, hiding her fierce blushes beneath the brim of her hat, she felt tiny tremors attack every inch of her body as he reached out and removed her battered headgear, setting her long silky blonde hair tumbling around her face.

'There is nothing to be ashamed of in being hot on a day such as this.' His voice curled with amusement as he leaned forward and curled his tongue around the beads of perspiration dewing the beginnings of the valley between her breasts.

Bonnie shuddered in response to the current of fire arrowing to the most secret part of her, and she had to call on all her dwindling reserves of self-preservation to stop her hands from lifting to that well-shaped dark head to hold him exactly where he was. A moan—part shame, part exultation—was torn from her as his tongue dipped, just lightly, tantalisingly, beneath the V of her neckline. And then he lifted his head, and she encountered the glint of wickedness in his black-as-sin eyes and wondered what was stopping her from slapping him for taking uninvited liberties.

Deplorable lust was stopping her, she mourned, wanting him to touch her again and hating herself for it.

Her skin was still tingling and tightening as he stated, in a voice full of high-voltage masculine knee-trembling authority, 'We shall cool down in the sea.'

Bonnie shook her head in a vain attempt to clear it. Why was she letting him call all the shots? Touch her so intimately? Did he regard her as a fluff-headed bimbo with no mind of her own? Was he so typically a Greek macho male that he looked on all nubile females as mere playthings, simperingly anxious to please?

Calling on her professional authority, she cleared her throat edgily before managing to remind him, 'We're here, as I recall, to discuss your progress in locating Dimitri Kyriakis. And we're wasting time.'

Her pride in her ability to disregard the way he made her feel and get down to business took a sharp nosedive as he sprang lithely to his feet.

'Later. Join me in the sea.'

'I—'

'Later.'

Momentarily his smile dazzled her, made her heart turn over. And then she felt frustration at having her objection dismissed, as if whatever she might have had to say wasn't worth listening to. She took a deep breath, opened her mouth to categorically state that 'later' simply would not do, then closed it again—because he was already removing his T-shirt, revealing the torso that was hard, magnificent, packed with well-defined musculature, its slightly hair-roughened and sinfully touchable skin the colour of warm bronze.

He tossed the T-shirt aside, his eyes never leaving

hers, and his hands went to the waistband of his cargo pants, just below the taut muscles of his stomach. Every last gasp of breath left Bonnie's lungs.

CHAPTER FIVE

BONNIE swatted at a dive-bombing insect that seemed to have decided that tormenting her was to be its main aim in life for the forseeable future, and called herself seven kinds of fool.

Out there, deep in the cool, azure sparkling ocean, Stavros was cleaving through the water towards the rocky headland. Despite what she had mentally termed his X-rated striptease, which had made her mouth run dry and her heart bump like a steam hammer, he'd emerged from her self-inflicted erotic fantasy perfectly respectable in black boxer shorts.

Well, sort of—if you could call six foot plus of bronzed, almost naked magnificent manhood something as tame as merely 'respectable'.

Even so, she'd squirmed with an uncomfortable mixture of primal lust and plain old-fashioned common sense when he'd given her that slow, sexy smile and invited again, 'Join me?'

Doing her best, she'd shaken her head and arranged her features into what she'd hoped was a mask of polite indifference. She'd tacked on, 'No, thanks,' for good measure, and watched him simply shrug his wide shoulders and walk away over the hot white sand towards the curling line of foam where the sea met the shore. She had realised, belatedly, that she'd probably only succeeded in looking ridiculously prissy, while at the same time condemning herself to sweating and sweltering in the fierce afternoon heat, when the cool, sparkling blue waters of the placid ocean lay so temptingly close.

It was not in her character to cut her nose off to spite her face, she reminded herself firmly, getting to her feet and slipping off her shorts. Clad in her vest top and a pair of flower-patterned briefs, she was just as respectable as he was!

And she didn't have to swim with him, did she? The vast expanse of water was big enough for them both to cool off, without actually having to set eyes on each other or get close enough to touch.

At the thought of touching him her heartbeat quickened. So she wouldn't think about it, she lectured herself crossly as she sped over the baking sand and flung herself into the shallows with relief.

As the cool waters closed around her Bonnie made every effort to dig out some common sense from the mess her brain seemed to have got itself in.

Useless to get in a state and allow her wretched, hitherto reasonably dormant hormones to get the better of her.

She had to slot this morning's events into context.

Stavros was clearly a man who decided on a course of action and stuck to it. Rigidly. There was nothing devious in the way he was stalling. They would eat. They would take a cooling dip in the ocean. And then they would discuss the whereabouts of Dimitri Kyriakis. In that order.

So she'd go with the flow—his flow—and forget the way he affected her physically. Put it out of her mind along with her feelings of frustration about the way he was stalling about the information she needed regarding Andreas's son. Although it was a frustration that made her want to jump up and shake him, and put together they promised imminent mental derangement!

She wasn't normally a lustful woman, she reminded herself sensibly. So this fit of physical madness had to be down to his undeniably fantastic looks, the hot Greek sun and the beautiful island surroundings.

During the four years of their engagement she had never once been tempted to jump on Troy and smother him with kisses—and he had been her fiancé, for goodness' sake! In fact their physical contact had been pretty low-key, now she came to think of it, and she'd refused point-blank to move in with him before marriage, stating that she believed in waiting for their wedding night.

Keeping well within her depth, she struck out, following the curving shoreline. She was a graceful swimmer, but not a strong one, and it wasn't long before she decided to wade back to the shore— because for the past few minutes the current had strengthened, and she was making zero progress and tiring rapidly.

Failing to find a foothold on the sand bottom, she realised with a stab of shock that she was now out of her depth and she panicked, recognising for the first time that just here the placid surface of the sea was pockmarked with what appeared to be mini-whirl-pools.

Arms flailing uselessly, she felt the undertow tug at her legs, and a sob of relief burst inside her chest as she saw Stavros, his powerful crawl bringing him closer with every second. Within moments he was beside her, a strong arm around her waist as he bit out, 'Relax. I have you,' and kicked out for the shore.

In what seemed like no time at all he'd set her on her feet in the shallows. Her legs felt like cotton wool, and embarrassment at her wimpish, girly be-haviour when she'd thought she was drowning en-gulfed her. To hide the humiliation she was cowering beneath, she quipped, 'Do you make a habit of rescuing damsels in distress?'

Just for a moment she saw his eyes go hard and black, and then he flashed that slow, sensual smile of his as he countered, 'No, but I could get to enjoy it.'

The look in his eyes told Bonnie he was making the most of the situation, subjecting her dripping, scantily clad body to overt male appreciation—just before the hands that had been at her waist, steadying her, lowered to her hips and tugged her against the evidence of his hard arousal. Bonnie gasped as shocking excitement claimed her.

She snatched in a ragged breath, and met the knowledge, the searing intimacy in his glinting dark eyes. She felt her legs turn to jelly as he breathed, 'I need to claim my reward,' and took her mouth with a tantalising gentleness that set her head spinning.

Her lips parted involuntarily beneath the teasing warmth of his, inviting more, wanting more, needing more. Her full breasts pressed with telling urgency against the wall of his naked chest, and it wasn't until he straightened, setting her a pace away from him, that she realised with deep embarrassment that her hands were clutching his wide, muscular shoulders as if her life depended on keeping him close.

She had to hand it to him, though, she thought in deep misery, as she followed him back to the shade of the olive tree, the sand burning the soles of her feet with every stumbling step she took. He could have done anything with her and he must have known it.

Of course he'd known it! He wasn't wet behind the ears!

Even now, with humiliation washing over her, her breasts still tingled and there was an ache between her thighs. She'd been gagging for it!

The horrible phrase shamed and chastened her so much that her stomach churned sickly.

But on the upside—and the optimist in her sought to find one—she had to be thankful that he hadn't taken advantage of her as he could so easily have done. Because, far from objecting, she knew to her disgust she would have actively encouraged him!

She'd never had this sort of reaction to any man in her life, and she didn't like it one little bit! She who was always in control seemed to lose it around this spectacular guy, she mourned, plodding on. She seemed to have precious little will-power with which to fight her attraction to him. He'd kissed her and she'd ignited, her apology for a brain suffering complete and utter burn-out.

Reaching the shade minutes before her, Dimitri turned, watched her. Pure poetry in motion. He flattened out an incipient self-deprecating grin, amazed at his first ever slide into inanity.

But, he excused himself, she *was* the most beddable woman he'd ever encountered! Water drops glistened on her warmly tanned skin, wet hair dripped on to her smooth shoulders, and her vest clung to her upper body like a second skin, the circles of her nipples standing proud. And the now near transparency of her briefs left very little to the imagination.

Beddable—and she knew it.

And she was playing a subtle game. Not for her the full-on seduction technique to get the information she needed out of him. She was using far more oblique tactics.

Starting with her initial refusal to join him in the water, her expression that of a prim maiden aunt. Then her rapid change of mind, keeping an eye on his whereabouts before getting into 'difficulties', ensuring that he had no option but to go to her rescue.

A cynical opinion? Maybe. But life and experience had made him that way. And it would take a damn sight more than a pair of limpid smoke-grey eyes fringed with fabulous golden-tipped lashes to make him change his take on beautiful women who simpered around him and likened him to a knight in shining armour.

Testing, he'd kissed her. And he had his answer. His body had urged him on, wanting to take the whole thing further—much further—but the mind that was always in total control had him stepping away from her just as she upped a gear, that warm, utterly fantastic body squirming suggestively against him, her hands holding him, lips parting with hungry demand.

Had her need to do a wealthy old man's bidding had her sticking to that old chestnut to 'lie back and think of England'? Or had that hot response been real? Was she *that* highly sexed?

The latter, he decided as she stood before him. She was a true voluptuary—a woman who would use her fantastically gorgeous body to get a life of luxury and sensual pleasure. For why else would she be holed up with a man old enough to be her father, and then some, if it wasn't for what she thought she could get from him?

'Tell me why you're so anxious to locate Dimitri Kyriakis, Bonnie.'

The sound of her name, softly spoken in that sensual rough-velvet slightly accented voice, sent shivers down her spine. He was leaning oh, so casually against the gnarled trunk of the tree, his arms crossed over his chest.

Horribly aware of his long lean body, the sheer male beauty of the man, she avoided the dark intensity of his eyes. She felt something hot quiver and coil deep inside her, and grabbed the lifeline his words offered.

Get the information she wanted from him and she need never see him again—would make *sure* she never saw him again.

She could recognise danger when it stared at her with dark, compelling eyes, and if she knew herself—and she was sure she did—she could make the effort to finally get her act together and run a mile just as soon as she had what she wanted from him.

Her mind fizzing, she bent to snatch her discarded shorts from where she'd dropped them earlier and pulled them on, her fingers fumbling with the zip. He was, she knew, probably her last hope of locating Andreas's son, and she would have to tell him as much as she could without breaking any confidences.

'You might as well be comfortable while you tell me.' He indicated the soft dry earth beneath the tree with a brief, decisive flick of a hand. 'Sit.'

Glancing up at his lean, golden honey-toned features, Bonnie bit down hard on her soft lower lip, a shiver racing down her spine. There had been a change—a fleeting one, admittedly, but definitely there. In the tone, in the expression of cool authority—almost arrogance.

She sat, because it seemed counter-productive to refuse, her legs tucked up beneath her, and watched as he emptied what was left in the wine bottle into the glass she'd used earlier and handed it to her.

He sat beside her, long bronzed legs stretched out before him. He might look relaxed, but wary tension curled inside her. She was sure he could tell her what she wanted to know, but how much did she dare to reveal?

Just the basic facts, she decided, pushing a rapidly drying lock of hair away from her face with the back of her hand. 'I have a message for him from his father,' she stated baldly. And then, because some elaboration was probably called for, she stressed, 'It's a message I just *know* he'll be wanting to receive.'

Interesting.

Dimitri watched her expressive features closely. She sounded—looked—amazingly earnest, as if the passing on of this so-called message was important to her. And to his father, of course. Mustn't forget him. That his father had sent his woman to track him down had never been in doubt. He was always right. It wasn't in his nature to make mistakes. She had just confirmed it, albeit unnecessarily.

But it wasn't enough. It would take far more than the vague promise of a message—which, if it existed, and he doubted it, would take the form of a plea to back off, leave him with *something* of his once strong business empire—for him to divulge his true identity.

His initial assessment that his father had dispatched the beautiful Bonnie to make contact with him, to use her considerable assets to seduce his future plans from him, was the right one.

The old man was playing games. Dimitri almost admired him for that. But two could play games. And to allow Bonnie to discover his true identity would mean that his father would win this battle. And that would not happen.

He'd despised the man who'd sired him after that abortive attempt to get help for his sick mother when he'd been fourteen years old, hated him since the needlessly early death of his mother—a demise that could have been postponed by several years if the mega-wealthy Andreas Papadiamantis had had an ounce of compassion or common humanity.

He'd vowed to take revenge. He'd succeeded. Won every move in the game. He wasn't about to lose this one.

'And the message is?' he coaxed gently, watching

the long, gold-tipped lashes lower over sexily smoky big grey eyes as the soft corner of her lush mouth was caught between her teeth.

She shook her lowered head. Reluctantly. She'd make a damn fine actress. He smiled.

'It's private, Stavros. Between Dimitri Kyriakis and his father.' Her eyes pleaded. 'Please understand.'

She couldn't go blurting out all that personal stuff to a virtual stranger. Apart from confidentiality, how could she know that Stavros wouldn't blurt out whatever information she gave him to all and sundry? It was a close-knit community, and while it was tight-lipped to outsiders on the subject of the whereabouts of the man she had to find, she was sure information and gossip was shared freely between them.

Suddenly awkwardly aware of the glass she'd forgotten she was holding, she lifted it, tempted to pour the contents onto the dry ground. But that would look ungraciously rude, and would make him even more reluctant to help her than he already seemed to be. There was no way she could afford to do that.

He watched as she drained the wine he'd given her. The movement of her lovely throat was fascinating. She set the glass aside. Her pouting mouth was slick from the wine. The instinct to taste those inviting lips was intense.

He said, his voice strangely thickened as the

intent formed in his mind, 'If Dimitri is a friend of mine, and you are a friend of his father, and you and I are friends—yes?—then we are together, and a solution to the impasse may be found.'

Allowing her to absorb that, he stacked the used glasses, dishes and the remains of the picnic back in the cool box. When that was done, he tossed lightly over his shoulder, 'I will take you back to the good Athena and call for you at eight this evening. We will have supper together and talk the matter over more thoroughly than I have time for right now. Yes?'

Who was setting out to seduce whom to gain information? Dimitri picked up the cool box and grinned, extending a hand to help her to her feet.

Role reversal.

He liked it!

CHAPTER SIX

SHE was going to let him give her supper, but it wasn't a date—not what you'd call a proper date. More like a business thing, really.

The thought was uncomfortable, but Bonnie couldn't help wondering if Stavros would ask for money in return for the information she was sure he had. She caught her breath, stopping that line of thinking in its tracks, because she found the idea that he might be that kind of man so distasteful it made her heart twist heavily inside her breast.

Dropping her hairbrush down on the small cupboard that served as a nightstand and dressing table, Bonnie stared with disgust at the band of freckles across her nose in the face reflected back at her from the small mirror above it. How much did she really know about him? Very little. For all she knew Stavros was simply stringing her along. But she had no option but to agree to spend the evening with him on the off chance that he would help her.

Refusing to be negative, because that would get

her nowhere, she selected a sleeveless cream-coloured blouse from the hanging rail which was the only storage on offer in the basic accommodation and slipped it on over her lacy bra. The row of tiny pearly buttons going down from the V neckline was hidden behind pretty pintucks. Wondering why she was bothering to doll herself up, when her evening would be spent in one or the other of the island's two very rustic tavernas, she teamed it with a knee-length tawny cotton skirt and stepped into bronze-coloured strappy sandals.

A dab of her favourite cologne and she was satisfied that she looked as good as was possible—given her far from model-like proportions and those freckles. She wondered at the wriggle of excitement deep in her tummy. It was because this evening promised to be a turning point, she told herself as she picked up her purse. Nothing whatever to do with the fact that she would be spending a few hours with the most gorgeous man she had ever laid eyes on.

He had admitted that he knew Dimitri Kyriakis, that they were actually friends. And if he wasn't telling porkies then that was a huge step forward. And who knew? He might have already contacted his friend, told him about her and the message she had from his father and asked if he would agree to meet her.

Her mood swinging away from doubt and ugly suspicion, she left her room and rapidly descended the narrow twisting staircase on an optimistic high. She'd soon find out—and if a meeting *had* been set up she'd have to do her best to be polite and non-judgemental towards the man who had so callously set out to ruin his aged father. Even now, frail as he was, Andreas could be pacing the floor, waiting to hear from her that her message had been delivered and a happy outcome could be expected.

On time, Bonnie stepped out into the silkily warm darkness. Down at the harbour the ferry, ablaze with twinkling lights, was docking—later than usual due to the tides, she supposed.

If things had gone without a hitch earlier she might have been returning to the mainland in a couple of hours or so on that very ferry, to spend her last week in Greece visiting Athens and doing the tourist bit before returning home to help her mother with the anniversary party preparations.

Lost in her thoughts, she gave a jerk of surprise as a gleaming four-by-four drew up on the narrow street and Stavros leaned over and opened the passenger door. There was a note of wry amazement in his voice as he said, 'So I have the pleasure of escorting a woman who doesn't believe it's fashionable to be late. Hop in.'

He sounded as though he knew all about the fashionable set—society ladies who tinkled with sycophantic laughter or pouted with sultry invitation, depending on which button was being pressed, Bonnie thought as she clambered into the passenger seat. But he was an island odd-job man, or whatever, and that simply couldn't be true.

Though, looking at him—white shirt gleaming against warm olive-toned skin, dark hair smooth against his well-shaped head, mature tough features, sharply angled cheekbones, the fine blade of his nose above a mouth that could be sensual and commanding at one and the same time—she found it possible to believe he *could* slot easily into the rarefied circle of the world's movers and shakers, a prime target for circling predatory females.

Dismissing such flights of fantasy, and wishing that the tense wriggle of excitement hadn't taken residence inside her the moment she was in his company, she articulated the first thing that came into her head as she settled back into the luxuriously soft leather upholstery.

'I was expecting your old buggy.' Or, more likely, for him to have parked the rattly contraption and met her on foot, because neither of the tiny town's two tavernas was more than three minutes' walk away from where she was staying.

It was a remark he chose to ignore, merely putting the engine into gear and easing down the narrow street. They passed the harbour and the lined-up parked vans waiting to collect supplies and the straggle of foot passengers disembarking from the ferry, looping round and passing between the pretty colour-washed little houses that clung to the hillside, to link up again with the island's only proper road.

Finding the silence distinctly unsettling, Bonnie broke it. 'Where are we going?'

'Back to where I first found you.'

His profile gave nothing away. His lean, strong hand on the gear lever was so beautiful it made her heart turn over, made her voice thick as she posed, 'Your boss's place? Won't he mind?'

'He is delighted that I should have the company this evening of a beautiful woman,' Dimitri gave her, without a hint of the amusement that welled inside him at the anticipation he was attributing to another man. He was looking forward to the evening ahead. He had no interest whatsoever in his father's message. But he found, to his own quiet amazement, that he wanted to discover what made Bonnie Wade tick.

The women in his life had been treated generously and with respect while he had use of them. No more than that. He had never wanted to find out what went on inside their artfully lovely heads. He was a sexual cynic, he decided wryly.

That the woman beside him right now was different could only be down to her relationship to his enemy, he rationalised.

Something hot had kicked deep inside Bonnie's tummy when he'd referred to her as being beautiful. She felt her cheeks flush with pleasure, and was glad the darkness hid her gaucheness. Such a compliment, paid to her by a man for whom the description could have been invented, did loads for the self-esteem that

had been on the floor since she'd been so ignominiously dumped by Troy; hidden, unacknowledged,
but there—a fact she was only now properly recognising.

Swinging off the road, the vehicle slowed, its
headlights picking out a track hugging a high stone
wall, and a pair of ornate iron gates ahead, that
swung respectfully open at their approach.

'The frontage of the villa,' Dimitri explained as
the wheels crunched over immaculately raked fine
gravel. 'From here we walk. Just a little way. We
dine in the gazebo. Everything is ready.'

The real Stavros had followed Dimitri's instruc-
tions to the letter, and although his manservant/body-
guard hadn't been happy about it he'd consented to
make himself scarce for the night—whether a sneak
invasion of the media, anxious for compromising
shots of the mega-rich at play took place tonight or
not.

The moon had risen, and the torch he'd taken from
the four-by-four was redundant as he took her hand
and led her down a path that wandered through flow-
ering shrubs, releasing their perfume into the silvered
night.

As the path widened into a grassy glade Bonnie's
fingers tightened around the firm warmth of his
hand. 'That's so beautiful!' she gasped, awestruck
at the sight of the soaring pale marble columns sup-
porting an octagonal building that looked almost
ethereal in the cool moonlight.

Marble steps led up to the marble-paved interior. She could hear the soft, almost hypnotic murmur of the sea, but couldn't see it. Tall candles illuminated the eight-sided room, revealing wide padded banquette seating against each wall, upholstered in dark blue fabric and covered with cushions in jewel shades. The centre of the room held a low table set with silver and crystal, and what appeared to be a lavish cold buffet.

Magical… But—

'Are you sure our being here's OK?' Bonnie glanced up at him uneasily. She knew nothing whatsoever about his employer, or Stavros's employment status—whether or not his use of this sophisticated and sumptuous place was a perk of his job. A frown pulled her brows together. She would hate to think that he was trying to impress her, making free with the place in his boss's absence.

And yet he was so commandingly handsome, his crisp white shirt tucked into the waistband of beautifully tailored trousers that hugged his narrow hips and long legs to perfection, he didn't give the impression of being a humble odd-job man.

Looking into his devastatingly gorgeous features, the candlelight gilding the impressive angles and planes, she marvelled that she hadn't seen it before: the stamp of authority on those lean, dark, charismatic features, the way he held himself, self-confident to the point of arrogance. Her earlier impression that he was a laidback sexy odd-job man, fated like the rest of the male population of this insular little island to pick up a living as best he could until he reached an age when he would join the old men who sat in the square or outside the tavernas grumbling, vanished like morning mist beneath the rays of a strengthening sun.

'Relax.' The warmth, the assurance of his voice curled around her, and his hand rested on the base of her spine to urge her further into the room. 'I have the owner's full permission and encouragement to be here.'

The touch of his hand was setting up a chain reaction inside her. Perversely, she wanted him to stop touching her. Yet the desire to feel his hands all over her tingling body was even stronger.

Never before had she had the hateful feeling of being indecisive. In her professional life she'd always known what she wanted and had gone for it with single-minded determination—and that had rubbed off on her personal life, too. She'd rarely dated because she'd spent all her free time studying to further her career, to get where she wanted to be.

Only once had she made a wrong call. When Troy's persistence and her mother's gentle warnings about women who were wedded to their careers and grew old without the joys of children and family life had led her to think things over and agree to accept Troy's proposal.

And look where *that* had got her!

They had reached the luxuriously upholstered

banquette. Dimitri removed a cushion, eased her down, and placed the cushion comfortably behind her back. She was as tense as a fawn scenting the approach of a hunter.

Time to change that.

'Relax,' he repeated, in that same nerve-tingling tone as he settled beside her. Too close. 'I believe we will enjoy one another's company.'

Too much for her peace of mind! Enjoying him wasn't what she was here for! She swallowed down a gulp of sheer panic, smoothed her skirt over clamped-together knees and said as firmly as she could manage, given that every last one of her senses was screaming as he brushed the fall of her hair away from her face, the backs of his fingers brushing her sensitised skin, 'You say you know Dimitri Kyriakis—?'

'Very well. You might say intimately.' His lips curved as he saw the sudden jerk of her head, met the determination, the hope, in those seductive smoke-grey eyes, and he deflected her. 'First a little champagne. And then, after a while, I promise I will try to forget that I am in a secluded, romantic setting with a lovely woman I aim to get to know much better, and I will force my mind into less fascinating channels and talk about what you want to know.'

And he would tell her nothing. Zero. His enemy wouldn't get to him through her. The liquid bubbled into two flutes and he set the bottle back on its nest of ice. And yet he was undeniably attracted to her.

Because she was an enigma? Because he wanted to solve the puzzle of why a beautiful woman with apparently everything going for her should hook up with an old man—a cruel, uncaring man?

He handed her a glass of the pale golden wine. Solve the enigma and the attraction would disappear.

Or would it?

As he retook his seat beside her, his long, hard-muscled thigh touched hers. Her face burned. All that smooth-tongued talk about romantic settings and getting to know her better had turned her to mush, even though she knew he was only using the patter of a serial flirt.

And he was far too close. But she wanted him to be closer. Much. The heavy tingling in her breasts, the heat flaring deep inside her, told her that much.

Silly, silly woman!

Why didn't she tell him—with dignity—that unless they got down to the nitty-gritty she would leave and continue her search on her own?

Because so far on her own she'd got nowhere. And that wasn't going to alter during the time she had left.

Why hadn't she advised Andreas to hire a private detective, to track his son down and deliver his message?

Because she hadn't thought of it. Too determined to do what she could to help a deeply troubled, wronged, nice old man. Miss Fix-it! Miss Goody-Two-Shoes! she thought with self-disgust, and swallowed the cool, delicious contents of her glass.

The bubbles tickled the back of her nose, and the sudden assault of alcohol on her empty tummy cleared her head—or at least she told herself it did.

Why was she getting her knickers in a twist?

Stavros was flirting—he probably couldn't help it. It was the sort of harmless, meaningless game people less buttoned-up than she played all the time—nothing to get hot and bothered about. And he *had* promised to tell her where to find Andreas's son. Hadn't he? Her nose wrinkled in her effort to remember exactly what he'd said.

Surely, as a grown, successful woman, she had enough self-control to stop herself from doing what her wretched hormones craved and throwing herself at him?

He eased himself to his feet, his eyes never leaving hers, holding her, and refilled her glass. Easing herself luxuriously back against the cushions, relaxing against all her expectations, Bonnie smiled softly and shook her head. Already she felt a little bit swimmy. 'I don't want any more.'

The glass was placed back on the table. Bubbles danced in the crystal flute. He sat beside her, his thigh burning against hers, those wide shoulders, clad in the coolest white cotton, angled towards her. She could smell him. The warmth, the clean, heady maleness of him, the faint tang of a lemony cologne.

He was everything a woman dreamed of. Male perfection. Tall, dark and handsome—and yet so much more. Toe-curlingly sexy. Formidable.

If he wanted to flirt with her—or more—then what was wrong with that? She could recall the way some of her colleagues had boasted about holiday romances. Apparently it happened all the time.

Fun. Fun was all it was.

And what was the harm in a few kisses?

She craved his kisses.

Didn't she deserve to let her hair down for once, after the humiliation Troy had dealt her?

Every last nerve-end in her body was screaming for his touch, his lips on hers, his hands touching her. Her body had always responded to him. It had an indomitable will of its own when he was around.

'Tell me, Bonnie…' His hand cupped the side of her face, long fingers idling through her hair, making her soft lips part on a decidedly shaky intake of breath. 'Tell me what you *do* want?'

CHAPTER SEVEN

SHE didn't need to give a verbal answer. Her body language spoke for her.

Dimitri lowered the thick fringes of his sable lashes over the silver glint in his dark eyes.

His enemy had chosen his messenger well. A man less single-minded would have been putty in her hands—would have done anything, given up the secrets of his very soul, to possess the bounty of such a woman.

She'd been blessed with a body of such sensuousness that the very air around her throbbed with it. It was palpable—a magnet for male attention.

He wasn't immune—far from it. But putty in a woman's hand—in *anyone's* hand—he wasn't.

The tightening of his groin foretold the immediate future with an accuracy he'd be a fool to try and deny. If she was offering, he wouldn't be resisting.

How could he?

His hand moved. Fingertips rested lightly on the corner of her mouth. He felt the soft warm flesh tremble, just slightly, and as he slowly ran the pad of his thumb over her voluptuous mouth her lips parted invitingly. Elation stabbed him.

He had her!

Slowly, and with devastating intent, he lowered his dark head and moved his hand beneath her silky silvery hair, curving it around the tender nape of her neck. His lips parted as he took hers, their exploration slow and gentle at first, until he registered her helpless groan. And then his mouth ravished hers, his tongue a thrust of explicit intent, his hand dropping to curve instinctively around one magnificent, straining, engorged breast, feeling the weight, the heat, as heat echoed and intensified in his loins.

And as she raised her arms to wrap them over his shoulders, her head thrown back, exposing the lovely length of her throat, her fantastic body moving sensuously against him, he felt an excitement such as he'd never known before. It took all control out of his hands and tossed that valuable commodity to the four winds, to be blown away on a gale of previously unknown hedonistic pleasure.

Bonnie gave vent to a tiny gasp of wonder as he dropped lightly ravishing kisses along the length of her throat. Every cell in her body sang, and she felt as if she had never been fully alive before.

His lips came to rest in the hollow at the base of her throat, his fingers still moulding the heavy curve of her breast, forcing Bonnie to grasp his downbent head with both hands. Her fingertips dug through the thick, silky-soft dark-as-midnight hair to the hardness of bone beneath, hanging on for dear life, because she felt as if she were being swept away. Her body arched and strained against his with an eagerness she didn't even try to hide—because surely she'd been born for this moment?

She failed to realise that he'd dealt with the tiny buttons that secured her top and released the front fastening of her bra until her unfettered breasts sprang free. She cried out deliriously as his mouth trailed lower and his lips found her nipple and played with it. And then he was kissing her mouth again, his weight carrying her back against the cushions, his hands holding her arms above her head as she arched beneath him.

The heated depths of his kiss were so potent that she was lost in wild sensation, trembling with an overload of pleasure as his hands left her wrists to slide down over her shoulders, over the sensitised peaks of her breasts, settling against her taut midriff, his fingers stroking the tender flesh beneath the waistband of her skirt.

'You are exquisite.' The rough velvet of his voice was intoxicating. 'I want you as I have never wanted any woman before.' And that was the truth, plain and unvarnished, he thought on a fierce stab of pleasure. His enemy, who hadn't given him so much as a crust of bread when he'd needed help for his ailing mother, had now given him this spectacularly beautiful, excitingly responsive woman to enjoy!

'You skin feels like the finest silk,' he breathed, the air snagging in his lungs as she writhed beneath his touch, her hazy, drowning eyes holding his.

Flickering golden candlelight threw the angles and planes of his unforgettable features into fascinating relief, heightening the mystery of him, of what she felt for him. She couldn't get her head round it. Didn't want to try. Her brain was absent without leave and she didn't want it back. Not now. Because she knew what was going to happen next. And she wanted it to happen. Caution, even her hitherto strong sense of morality, weren't going to be allowed to spoil this wonder for her.

A few harmless kisses and a little flirtatious fun was the juvenile aim of an innocent. His touch, his kisses, had awoken her to what she truly was.

A woman. All woman. On the brink of awakening.

She lowered her arms from where he'd placed them and used her hands to draw his head back down to hers, her mouth locking onto his, accepting the hungry thrust of his tongue with passionate welcome. One of his hands dealt with the zipper at the side of her skirt and the other eased the cotton fabric aside, sliding across the slight curve of her tummy and lower, beneath the filmy lace of her briefs. He murmured low in his throat, something she couldn't hear properly, probably in his own language, and gently explored the damp heat of her. She squirmed under the expert invasion, unable to contain her greedy, wild response. Offering herself. All of herself.

* * *

She was almost asleep, sated, her lovely limbs tangled with his, the silky pale fall of her hair spread over the jewel shades of the cushions. The absolute beauty of her made his throat close up, and his heart stung with remorse at what he had privately named her before he'd discovered a truth that both shamed and deeply touched him in equal measure.

Bonnie Wade had been a virgin.

The shock of the discovery had stilled his driving thrust towards the pleasure this voluptuary could give him—the pleasure he'd craved with everything within him. But the distress of her, 'Don't stop!' and the way she'd lifted her hips and wrapped her legs over his had been an invitation impossible to resist.

This lovely lady was no career mistress, selling her body to the highest bidder, moving onwards and upwards to reach her ultimate goal: a gold wedding ring, no matter how old and cranky the giver, provided he was wealthy. As Andreas Papadiamantis continued to portray himself as being.

He had wronged her. Unforgivably. Somehow he must make amends.

The touch of his fingers against the side of her face had those long, gold-tipped lashes lifting. Her smoky eyes were dreamy and her smile was beatific as she turned her head to press her lips into the palm of his hand.

'Stavros—'

'Hush, *pethi mou*. Later.' Curling his hand beneath her chin, he turned her head and brushed the lightest of kisses against her parted lips. He felt her immediate response and swung his feet to the marble floor.

It would be so easy to hold her through the night, make love to her again and again, but self-gratification came low on his list of priorities when there were more pressing matters to attend to.

His prime objective at this moment was to discover the true nature of her relationship with his father—how she lived, what she wanted from life. And, most importantly, why a woman such as she—beautiful, sensuous, warm and giving—should have remained a virgin, only to surrender that state to a virtual stranger she believed to be a casual odd-job man. A man who might or might not have orchestrated a date—complete with a useless promise to give her information she needed—because he believed that female English tourists were fair game.

Only then could they move on.

Extricating his trousers from the scattering of jettisoned garments, he pulled them on and dealt with the zipper in short order. Then he took out this new and alien development and looked at it more closely.

Never before had such a need to know more claimed him where a woman was concerned. He'd had a handful of affairs—all relatively short-lived and devoid of any real emotion. The benefits to both sides had been clearly stated and understood, the parameters precisely laid out and strictly adhered to. Step out of line and the woman concerned would be history.

He had had no interest in the life or background of any of the females who had at the time shared a small part of his life. Good manners had decreed that he asked her preference in eating places, or in her choice of venue for the occasional short break—Alpine chalet or luxury yacht—but that had been as far as it had ever gone.

He plucked an afghan from the end of the banquette, the long line of his mouth determined as he took it back to where she still lay amongst the cushions. Taking her hands in his, he pulled her upright and carefully wrapped her lush body in the fine woollen fabric.

She felt like a parcel. Bonnie's grin was pure mischief as she wondered when he would be tempted to unwrap her again. Lying there, in what she could only describe as a state of bliss, watching him as he dressed, his body the epitome of male perfection, perfectly proportioned, strongly muscled yet full of grace, she wondered if this was what falling in love was like.

She'd been fond of Troy, had admired his work ethic, understood his strong practical streak, and believed he would make a good husband and father. But she had refused to move in with him before the wedding because—and she could now be honest with herself—the thought of sharing a bed with him hadn't lit any fires for her.

With Stavros it was different. Tonight she'd thrown caution to the wind. Always practical—show her a career nurse who wasn't!—she'd never once made a decision that wasn't sensible. Thrill-seeking was not for her. But now it was as if, she thought dreamily as Stavros sat back amongst the cushions and pulled her down beside him, she had long been asleep, waiting for the magical touch of one special man to awaken her to the full glory of her womanhood.

With a little sigh of something that went far deeper than mere contentment, Bonnie snuggled her head into the wide span of his shoulder, felt his arm tighten around her for a moment, and heard the warmth of his voice as he leaned forward.

'We eat—talk a little. We have shared something very special, and I find I want to know many things about you.'

'OK.'

Although she felt she knew all she needed to know about Stavros—all that was important, anyway—the fact that he wanted a potted life history had to mean that he didn't simply regard her as a one-night stand, another notch on his bedpost, someone to be easily enjoyed and just as easily forgotten—didn't it?

His voice had a husky quality that made her toes curl as, having made his selection, he handed her a plate. '*Mezedhes*—the chicken and fish have been grilled and chilled.' He indicated the appetising morsels on cocktail sticks. 'Vegetables, too. And try the *baklavas*—honey and nut pastry—you will enjoy them.'

Surprisingly, Bonnie had found her appetite. Although she would have said, if asked, that she was too full of happiness to have room for anything else.

'So, tell me, how do you come to know the father of Dimitri Kyriakis?'

The question came as a shock. Not because he was curious—that was natural in the circumstances—but because she had completely forgotten why she had agreed to meet with Stavros this evening. The fact that he, and seemingly only he, could point her in the direction of the man she'd come to the island to find.

'Oh.' She licked the tips of her fingers and slid her empty plate back on the table. 'That's easy.' She named a prestigious private British nursing agency. 'I work through them. They gave me the assignment. I nursed him. I work in the remedial area. That means,' she explained, smiling up into his shadowed eyes, 'I move in, full-time, to care for patients who are recovering from life-threatening operations or illnesses until their practitioners give the all-clear and I'm no longer needed.'

'He was very sick?'

A little surprised by the remoteness of his tone, Bonnie gave back, 'Very.'

'And now?'

'Provided there is no recurrence of the cancer, he should do well.' Perhaps Stavros knew of his friend's long estrangement from his father? Hopefully, he too thought it time the rift was healed. That would explain the urgency she'd detected behind his last question.

Cancer. Dimitri strove to rationalise an alien sense of pity for the man he'd believed deserved no pity whatsoever. Twenty-four hours ago he would have been angered by the thought that his enemy could be taken from him by illness. Without his long-standing vendetta against the man who had so wronged his mother, callously abandoned her, uncaring of her fate, his life would have been empty.

But now, with what he felt—or was almost certain he felt—about the woman tucked so trustingly into his side, all he could feel was compassion for an old man who was sick and alone.

'You are close to him?' He dropped his head against the top of hers, which was now nestling into his shoulder again, resisting the impulse to lift her chin, smile into her eyes, kiss her.

'I try not to be—to stay professional,' Bonnie told him. 'Some patients can be cranky, full of self-pity or plain difficult, and that's understandable. But Andreas was none of those. He followed the diet and exercise and rest regime to the letter. I admired his determination to get strong again—sometimes people of his age simply give up, see no future—and then, when I discovered why he wanted to ensure he had a few more years left to him, I felt deeply sorry for him. That's why I agreed to find his son and deliver his message.'

'And that is?' Dimitri felt as if all the air in his lungs had frozen solid.

Bonnie hesitated, but only for a moment. She loved this man—she was sure she did. And where there was love, there was trust. One couldn't exist without the other. Besides, Stavros *knew* the elusive Dimitri Kyriakis—was his friend. Up to now he had jealously guarded his wealthy friend's privacy, and she had to admire him for that.

She twisted round to face him directly, the shawl slipping off one shoulder. 'There are things about his past he regrets deeply. Apparently his firstborn son died and the rift between them was never healed. And now he wants to end the estrangement between him and his younger son—your friend Dimitri. I don't know, but I imagine things were so bad between them that your friend changed his surname— perhaps to his mother's maiden name.' She was studying his expression, to see if she was making progress in the right direction, but how could she read anything into a block of stone?

Redoubling her efforts to get through to him, she explained, 'That's all the message is. Andreas wants to meet with his son, apologise for whatever he did to cause the rift in the first place, and see if they can find an understanding. Your friend can agree or not, as he pleases. It would be up to him. So—' she tried to keep the note of pleading out of her voice and failed '—will you tell me how I can get in touch with him?'

He'd been wrong in his initial cynical belief that his enemy had sent this woman to use her sexual expertise to wheedle his plans for his father's final downfall out of him. He freely admitted it.

Bonnie wasn't his father's woman. She'd been his nurse. And out of the goodness of her generous heart she'd agreed to deliver a message.

And she had ended up losing her virginity to the man she'd been sent to find! That didn't make him feel any better about himself.

He made his mind up with customary swiftness. The content of the message didn't surprise him. His father was nothing if not single-minded. Witness his determination to regain his health and strength, as described by Bonnie.

Andreas was down to his final few business assets. He would hang on to them by any means possible. A rapprochement between them would work in his favour—ensure that happened, that the dogs were called off.

But there didn't need to be a meeting, or an outpouring of hypocritical regrets, for that to happen.

The vendetta was off.

And his life—a better, gentler, far more meaningful and loving life—was about to begin.

With Bonnie?

He hoped so.

He would make it happen.

He pushed the tousled hair from her face—her lovely face. 'The message is as good as delivered.'

Now wasn't the time. But tomorrow he would tell
her who he was. That she might not forgive him was
something he refused to contemplate. It was too ter-
rifying to countenance. Earning her forgiveness,
telling her how he felt about her, would need more
time than they had right now.

'Tomorrow everything will be sorted out, I promise. I'll pick you up at Athena's at nine. Now…' He
took her hands and pulled her to her feet. 'Get
dressed. It's late. I'll take you home. And remember…' He cupped her face between his hands, his
eyes warm. 'We have something more than special,
and I don't aim to let it go.'

Suffused with a melting, warm flow, dizzy with
the earth-shattering events of the evening, Bonnie
scarcely had time to put her thoughts into any kind
of coherent order before he was handing her out of
the vehicle in front of Athena's house.

The warm darkness cocooned her. Only she and
Stavros existed. He touched her hands. Raised them
to his lips. She moved closer to him, prolonging the
moment, reluctant to part. The morning, when she
would see him again, seemed an eternity away.

'Bonnie—'

His voice was fractured as he took her mouth in a
deep, drugging kiss, and she was clinging helplessly
to him when Athena's giggle fractured the moment.

'Ah! There you are! I see you have found Dimitri
Kyriakis! A blessing—your questions were making

my head ache. Now, there is someone waiting to see you a long time. Please come.'

And she was gone, bustling back into the house, leaving a silence that hurt her ears. Bonnie's eyes widened. Took in the truth that was stamped on those handsome, stone-hard features.

She had never felt such a fool in her life! Never felt so hurt and wretched. How could she have trusted him? Believed she loved him?

For a moment she felt as if all the life had been frozen out of her.

And then her arm came up. She hit him. And with the sound of that well-earned slap ringing in her ears she stumbled into the house and slammed the door behind her.

CHAPTER EIGHT

BONNIE felt cheap. Used. Humiliated. But beneath it all, like an underground raging torrent, was anger. More anger than her body could contain.

And that full-bodied slap had relieved only a small fraction of it.

He'd led her by the nose.

Laughing at her!

Never correcting her when she'd called him Stavros.

Laughing at her!

Promising to help her locate Kyriakis.

Laughing at her!

Seducing her.

That she'd been an all-too-eager participant in that seduction made her feel totally sick!

He was nothing more than a vile, duplicitous devil! A man so mean-minded he would make it his life's work to ruin his own father because of a falling-out that had happened in the distant past.

A grudge-keeper.

The sort of man any right-minded woman would avoid like the plague. Nausea hit low in her stomach. She needed a shower, needed to scrub every last trace of him off her skin. But her feet felt super-glued to the floor tiles and her legs began to shake.

'So your business was personal—he was *happy* you found him!' Athena emerged from the kitchen, wiping her hands on a towel, her small black eyes dancing. 'Very happy, from what I saw!' Then her expression changed, became sombre. 'Dimitri Kyriakis would not be pleased to know that the man who is to be your husband is here, perhaps? He is not a man to be crossed. I warn you.'

Or slapped around the face by an enraged woman who was no fragile flower, Bonnie thought, on a tide of rapidly rising hysteria. She squashed it flat, brutally, and feeling more tired than she'd ever felt before, asked, 'What are you talking about?' That she had a husband-in-waiting was news to *her*!

'Mr Frobisher came on the ferry this evening to meet you.'

Troy! For pity's sake! She needed her ex-fiancé around like she needed an army of plague-carrying rats to visit her!

She listened, tight-lipped, as her hostess chattered on. 'He was lucky. I had a small vacant room for his use. But I am not comfortable. Dimitri Kyriakis is a powerful man, a good man, and he has done much for us here. Because of his generosity we have a clinic, a small school, and much more. He would not be happy to know I gave a room to his rival. Such a man as he does not deserve it.'

He deserved to be boiled in oil, Bonnie thought on a fresh tide of anger. A man who would deliberately hoodwink an honest woman, make her feel wonderfully special, seduce her and laugh at her behind her back—who would systematically set out to ruin his own father because of some juvenile sense of grievance—deserved a whole heap of bad things!

Making up her mind, she crossed to the foot of the stairs. She would not spend a moment longer than she had to on this island. She'd been used and humiliated, and if she saw that hateful man again she'd probably kill him!

'We'll get out of your hair as soon as we can, Athena. Do you know of anyone with a boat I could hire to take us to another island where we can wait for a ferry to get us back to the mainland?'

Athena's wrinkled face was suddenly wreathed in smiles. 'No need. The ferry did not leave. Some repair was needed. It will leave at eight in the morning. I will make sure you wake in time.'

Nodding her thanks, Bonnie mounted the stairs. The widow Stephanides couldn't wait to see the back of them, even if it meant forfeiting an extra week's payment for bed and board—money she could ill afford to lose. That vile man must have spectacular clout around here, she fulminated as she marched into her room.

Troy was stretched out on her narrow bed. He'd dumped her. End of story. What right had he now to muscle in on her space? Cause more problems? Ridiculously, she wanted to throttle him. She, who was normally the calmest, most even-tempered creature on the planet, was turning into a homicidal maniac—and all because of Dimitri Kyriakis!

'You took your time.' Troy's blandly good-looking face was sulky, his blond hair sticking up in tufts as he swung his legs off the bed. 'I've been waiting ages.'

'Why are you here?' Even to her own ears her voice sounded drained. She wanted nothing more than to shower in the tiny bathroom, crawl into bed and try to cleanse her mind of everything that had happened since Andreas's son had helped her down from the rocks.

'Sorry for grumping.' Troy ran his fingers through his rumpled hair. 'I didn't mean it to be like this. Only I've been run ragged,' he complained. 'I spoke to your folks—and that wasn't easy. But they finally agreed that I should put my side of the story to you, see if we could mend fences. So first I went to your place of work, and the old Greek guy told me where you were—once I'd explained our relationship. So here I came. I've been given a room that I swear must have been converted from an airing cupboard, small and horribly stuffy, and I didn't know where you were or when you'd be back.' He patted the empty space beside him on the bed. 'But we'll let that go—I want to talk to you.'

Bonnie ignored the invitation. The thought of sitting close to him made her shudder. She pulled out a hard wooden chair from behind the door and sat on it. 'We don't have a relationship,' she pointed out flatly. Not since he'd virtually left her at the altar. 'And I'm sorry your accommodation doesn't come up to scratch, but as we're leaving first thing in the morning it's not important.'

'But—'

'No buts. We're out of here. I need to shower and pack, but I'll give you ten minutes to explain what you're doing here.' She felt calmer now. All that destructive anger had ebbed out of her. She even admitted to a slight feeling of wonder. During all the time they'd been engaged she'd never spoken to Troy so positively. They'd rarely argued—perhaps only over the question of her moving in with him— other than that she'd accepted the status quo, agreed to decisions for the future—mostly Troy-led, she recognised from hindsight.

They would start married life in his flat, since she was to continue working and would be away quite a lot of the time. Save hard until they could afford a halfway decent house near to both his place of work and a good school, and then start a family. Two children—preferably one of each.

All safe and predictable. He earned good money, would make a good father to her children. But there'd been nothing 'meant' about their relationship. No passion.

Though as a sudden shafting pain twisted her heart to pieces, she decided that passion could go take a jump if the joy was more than equalled by the pain.

'So? Time's ticking,' she prompted. Her mouth felt stiff and wooden.

'Don't be like that!' Troy leaned forward, his arms resting on his thighs, his hands dangling between his knees. He cleared his throat awkwardly, as if reluctant to speak his mind.

And his apology was just a little grudging. 'I treated you shamefully, Bon. I know that. But—' there was an edge of accusation now, and his face turned turkey-red '—it wasn't all my fault. You wouldn't move in with me. You'd hardly let me touch you, even. So far and no further. I tell you, it was driving me mad. Then there was this girl at the office—a temp. She was giving off all the signals, and I was so frustrated I fell for it. We were seeing each other for a while and—I don't know—I hardly ever saw you, and when I did it was strictly hands-off, wait till we're married. Sandra knew how to please a man.'

'So you called the wedding off?' Looking back, she couldn't blame him—not really. And he was right. She did have to shoulder some of the blame for what had happened. Liking a guy, admiring his many good points, wasn't enough to base a marriage on. She should never have agreed to marry him.

Hindsight was a wonderful thing. She should have asked herself questions. His attempts at lovemaking, clumsy as she now knew from recent and shaming experience, had left her cold. She'd begun to believe that she might be frigid, and had hoped that everything would change once they were married. She should have asked herself then why, if Troy had needs, she was unwilling to satisfy them.

'It was crass of me,' he admitted into the uncomfortable silence. 'After a few months I realised that even if Sandra was great in bed she would make a rotten wife. Flighty, live for today with no thought for the future, not a sensible thought in her head. Look, Bon—' he spread his hands '—do me a favour. Let me make it up to you. It's you I really want. Can we start again?'

He looked like a puppy pleading for its dinner. She didn't have the heart to tell him that she might understand why he'd done what he had, but she had no intention of having anything to do with him in the future. She was in no fit state right now to make a sensible decision. And he had been honest, at least— which was more than could be said for some! And the way he'd succumbed to the siren Sandra was understandable, given the way she herself had drawn the line at anything more intimate than a kiss, a fairly chaste caress or two.

'I'll think about it,' she promised on a dredging sigh. Right now she felt too drained by events to take it any further. 'Now, we both have to get ready to leave first thing, so…' She tried a smile. It felt ill-fitting. 'I'll say goodnight.'

* * *

Bonnie was restless. This should have been her final week on that sun-drenched Greek island. Instead she was kicking her heels in the rambling former vicarage that had been her home for all her life. And it was a typical English summer. Raining.

It was too early to begin preparations for dinner, far, far too early to help her mother prepare for the anniversary party, and she wasn't due to contact the agency to see if they had a new assignment for her for at least another twelve days. The steady rain, more like a heavy mist, had put paid to her earlier intention to potter around in the garden, making good her promise to her dad to hoe between the rows of vegetables.

And her mum was at a community meeting, so there was no one to talk to. She needed to fill the space in her head with idle chit-chat because thinking made her feel wound up and fit to bust.

She felt so bad about herself.

That morning, two days ago, when they'd been waiting to board the ferry, Troy had been mildly grumbling ever since she'd woken him with a cup of coffee at seven. Still sounding hard done by, he'd objected, 'I was told you had another week here. As it is, I'm to get straight back on this wretched ferry, then hang about airports hoping for a flight. I don't know why you insist we leave now. We could have relaxed in the sun, sorted things out between us— after all, that is what I came for—'

He'd droned on, and bored by the repetitious

nature of his complaints she'd picked up her rucksack and shuffled forward. It had looked as though the foot passengers were beginning to board.

And then, not knowing why she did it, she glanced back over her shoulder. Sunlight was breaking through the morning mist, and it seemed to cast a halo of golden light around the tall, physically perfect specimen who was heading so purposefully towards them. She could even see the darkness that shadowed his tough jawline.

He looked as if he'd had a rough night.

She panicked. The only thought her spinning brain could come up with was to pay him back. Show the brute he hadn't hurt her—couldn't hurt her—that as far as she was concerned he'd been nothing more than an entertaining one-night stand.

Practically jumping into Troy's space, she'd hissed, 'Shut up! Kiss me!' and probably given him the shock of his life when she'd wrapped both of her arms around him and one of her legs and nearly swallowed him whole.

It had worked. When she'd finally extricated herself and furtively scanned the area there had been no sign of Dimitri Kyriakis.

But she shouldn't have done that. It hadn't been fair on Troy. She shouldn't have used him like that.

She should have let the vile man approach her, introduced him to Troy, listened to whatever reason he might have come up with for being down here at this time of the morning. Been dignified. Cool. Sensible.

It had taken the entire journey back to the UK—

ferry, road and air—to convince Troy that there was no future for them.

'What about that kiss?' he'd wanted to know. 'In front of everyone—not that I was complaining.'

'A rush of blood to the head. Sorry. I just wanted to find out if I felt anything.' *Lie!*

'And did you?'

'Sorry. No.' Absolute truth. 'Look, the plain fact is, I just don't respond to you physically, and that's something we should both have come to terms with long ago. I like you heaps—what's not to like!—but you deserve far better than that. Honestly you do. You'll make some woman a fine husband, but you have to see it can't be me. I'd make you miserable.'

So it had gone on, *ad nauseum*. The trouble with Troy was, once he got his teeth into something—the way she'd kissed him, in this case—he was like a terrier, worrying the subject to death.

She'd finally arrived home late last night, tuning into the gentle argument her parents had been having over mugs of cocoa. Her father, a busy GP, had suggested mildly that as the kids had all flown the nest they should sell up and move to somewhere smaller, easier to manage. Her mom had countered with the argument that the children always came back. 'Look at Bonnie—here. And Jake and Will turn up most weekends. Lisa when she can. And they'll all be here in the run-up to our party at the end of next week. If we lived in a small house, where would we put them?'

Finishing her own cocoa, Bonnie had said her fond goodnights. She knew her dad would never sell up; he loved his garden too much. He was always regaling whoever would listen with his plans for it once he was retired and had time on his hands.

Although their marriage was rock-solid, her parents enjoyed bickering. She supposed it must add a little spice to a relationship that had become as comfortable as an old pair of slippers.

She'd been lucky, brought up in a loving family, close-knit and caring. Unlike Andreas Papadiamantis, his wives and his sons. Apparently dysfunctional beyond belief.

The frail old gentleman had been the first thing on her mind when she'd woken this morning. She'd used her mobile to phone him from the privacy of her bedroom, to let him know his message had been delivered.

'How did he take it? Will he come? Did he say?'

Bonnie could detect the thread of anxiety in his voice, running beneath the relief.

'I expect he'll think it over.' What else could she say? That she hadn't asked him? Had almost taken his head off with the flat of her hand? That in her opinion a man who was a walking, talking grudge, intent on ruining his father, would ignore the message?

To her relief Andreas seemed to take that at face value, asking eagerly instead, 'Will you see my son again?'

'I'm back in England, so I doubt it.' If she never saw him again it would be too soon.

'Oh.' She could hear the disappointment in that solitary, tiny word, and felt even worse when Andreas gave an audible sigh and told her, 'I was hoping that when he came to see me, you would come, too. If anyone can pour oil on troubled waters it is you.'

'I don't think you'll need any help,' she said bracingly. Even though she was sure Kyriakis would ignore the needs of his father, she had to offer a slender thread of hope—because without hope what else was there? 'Just open your heart, tell him the things you told me, and you'll be fine.'

After enquiries as to his health and wellbeing, and extracting promises from him to stick to his exercise routine and the healthy diet she'd drawn up, she'd ended the call, promising to keep in touch, and felt truly miserable.

The sneaky devil who had made such a fool of her—seduced her and made her think for a brief space of time that she had found the one man she could love with all her heart, body and soul—would take no more notice of his father's message than he would of a falling leaf.

And now she was kicking her heels, fruitlessly wishing she could have really helped a frail, troubled man. Andreas so desperately wanted the opportunity to make amends for what he now realised was his shoddy earlier behaviour towards his family, to put things right between him and his remaining son. If Dimitri Kyriakis had been a different type of man—straightforward, with any hint of a capacity for forgiveness in his veins for a long-ago slight—there would have been hope for rapprochement between the two men.

As it was, the devious, self-centred devil would probably hold on to his grudge until his dying breath.

Deciding that she had to do something to take her mind off the way people made such a mess of their lives, she pressed her nose to the window and discovered that at last it had stopped raining. She pattered to the garden room to pick up the secateurs.

The ground was too wet to make hoeing possible, but here Dad had been complaining that the honeysuckle that covered the front porch was looking like something out of an untamed jungle, slapping everyone in the face as they tried to reach the door.

It was peaceful out here, the air deliciously fresh after the rain, and the mindless activity of clipping back and tossing the long, invasive tendrils into the waiting barrow to be taken to the compost bins was therapeutic. She had often heard her father say that at least fifty per cent of his patients would get far more benefit from an hour spent in the garden each day than any amount of pills, and she believed him.

She tugged a final wayward tendril down and reached up to clip it back, receiving a face full of water droplets. She made the final cut, smiling with satisfaction—until she heard the sound of an approaching engine.

Visitors. And look at the state of her. Old jeans, shabby shirt, hair all over the place. Pushing the secateurs into the pocket of her jeans, she used her fingers to wipe the spattering of water droplets from her face and ruefully hoped she didn't look as if she'd been dragged through a hedge. Her brows peaked as a sleek black Lexus swept round the final curve in the drive and pulled to a halt on the gravelled turning circle. No one around here drove a car like that.

The windows were tinted glass, so she had no idea who was behind the wheel until Dimitri Kyriakis emerged, his devastatingly and unfairly spectacular physique clad in the formal severity of a beautifully tailored dark suit, his shirt a dazzling white against the warm olive tones of his skin, his dark hair immaculate.

Intimidating, she thought in total shock. Every inch the hard-nosed businessman of legend. Nothing there of the laidback, casually dressed islander—the sultry-eyed, irresistible seducer.

Bonnie caught her bottom lip between her teeth, and the ground beneath her feet seemed to sway as he began to walk towards her, those dark eyes fastened on her, never leaving her. Goosebumps rose on her arms and she shivered. She lifted her chin. If it was payback time for that slap she'd delivered, then she was ready for him. She guessed no one had ever had the temerity to use physical violence against His High and Mightiness.

In the rarefied circles he obviously moved in, his minions—and that included his women—would go down on their knees and lick his shoes if he demanded it. But she wasn't one of them. In her book he didn't deserve one flicker of respect from her.

'What do you want?' Her chin titled higher as he stood in front of her and she collided head-on with those dark enigmatic eyes. There was no denying the beauty of those strong, lean features, but beauty was skin-deep and underneath he was pure poison.

'We have unfinished business.'

His voice had the same caressing warmth that she remembered. A shudder claimed her spine and something twisted in a knot deep inside her. But she wouldn't let herself remember the way she'd been so deeply attracted to him, how good his act had been, entrapping her, only once or twice giving her a glimpse of the mover and shaker he really was.

Almost idly he reached over and plucked a leaf from the bird's nest of her hair. The small glimmer of brightness in those midnight eyes warmed her.

'The streaked-with-mud look adds a certain piquancy.'

Bonnie gritted her teeth. She would not let him get to her, charm her away from her common sense again. She would *not*! And she wouldn't be tempted to do something stupid either—like hitting him!

'We have nothing to say to each other.' She held her ground even though his proximity and the clean scent of his aftershave had the effect of making her legs feel decidedly wobbly.

Her eyes flickered closed as he denied her. 'Wrong. And you *will* listen. May we go inside and conduct our conversation in more comfortable surroundings?'

Bonnie turned, defeated. But it was only a small setback, she attempted to console herself as she led the way through the house to the large family kitchen. She'd be damned if she'd show him to the sitting room—a graceful space, furnished with her mother's lovingly collected and cared-for antiques.

Stick him in the untidy, workaday kitchen. Treat him like a tradesman! Show him how unimpressed she was by his urbane elegance, his reputedly mega-standing in the world's business community.

Her shoulders rigid, she gestured to one of the hard wooden chairs ranged around the immense oak table and took the far more imposing Windsor chair at its head.

'Spit it out.'

He hadn't traveled this distance because he liked the colour of her eyes! Besides, there was one upside—she could take this unlooked-for opportunity to plead his father's case, point out that it wouldn't hurt him to at least listen to what the frail old man had to say. But she was totally unprepared for what came next.

'There are two things I must insist on.' His long legs stretched out in front of him, he looked as comfortable and as at ease as if he were reclining in a bespoke armchair rather than a hard old kitchen chair. 'Firstly, I need you to accompany me when I respond to the message you were so anxious to pass on and visit Andreas Papadiamantis tomorrow. My schedule is tight. You may have an hour to pack and let whoever may be interested know where you will be for the next week or two.'

And before she could spit out something really sophisticated, like *Go boil your head!* he dropped another bombshell in her lap. 'And you will stay right where I can see you—until I know for certain whether you are pregnant or not. I made the mistake of believing you to be experienced and protected.'

He dipped his head, just briefly, in acknowledgement of his error, and Bonnie felt her face crawl with embarrassed color as she was forced—internally kicking and screaming—to remember the heady passion of their lovemaking.

She didn't want to remember. Ever. But he punched it home with cool and deadly vengeance.

'Know this. If you are pregnant, then there is no way the life of a child of mine will be terminated. If you are pregnant I will marry you.' His inky black eyes entrapped her, scorched her, and her tummy looped alarmingly as he added, cool and smooth, 'That is not negotiable.'

CHAPTER NINE

'NEED me to hold your hand while you face Daddy?'

Contrary she might be, but Bonnie had had quite enough of being part of this sweetness and light charade—an uncomplaining, wimpy accomplice in Dimitri's devious pretence that everything was perfectly normal.

Her mother had turned up immediately after Dimitri Kyriakis had dropped his bombshell. It had exploded in Bonnie's mind, leaving her incapable of thinking straight, losing any hope of taking control of the situation. He had played the perfect gentleman, using that devastating smile and effortless charm to full effect. As he introduced himself as a friend, who also happened to be the son of the man she had so recently been caring for.

'And now he is asking for her—for us both, as a matter of fact. I'm sorry to drag Bonnie away so soon, but I hope you'll understand the need and forgive the intrusion. My father is a sick man.'

Fluttering beneath the battery of such easy charm,

her mother had done everything but actually give the smooth devil written permission to do whatever he wanted, shooing Bonnie away to do her packing while she gave their guest coffee and a slice of her walnut cake.

The only thing that had stopped Bonnie from digging her heels in and stating that she was going *nowhere* with him had been her recollection of her earlier phone call to Andreas, and the old gentleman's clear disappointment at discovering she was back in England and would not be around to sit in on the hoped-for meeting with his estranged son, to—as he'd put it—pour oil on troubled waters.

Ever since she'd tacitly agreed to accompany Dimitri she'd been treated like a princess, subject to every attention—whisked in leather-seated luxury to the airport, where his private jet had been waiting on stand-by, and then, once seated in what seemed more like a comfy armchair than the usual cramped airline seat, she'd been fussed over by a cabin crew for whom nothing seemed too much trouble.

It was ridiculous! Hence her catty remark now, clipped out as soon as he'd taken a sheaf of papers from his briefcase. Made just to let him know that she totally despised him and was only going along with this because she was fond of Andreas, whose delight at hearing Dimitri was willing to meet had been unprecedented.

'Holding hands would be nice,' he said, straight-faced, looking up from his reading material. 'I recall it, and other far more satisfying intimacies, very well.'

His dark eyes smouldered into hers, and Bonnie's face turned scarlet at the ungentlemanly reminder. Rage consumed her as his gaze dropped, lingering explicitly on the line of her throat exposed by the V-necked sweater she'd chosen to travel in, on the thrust of her breasts, and back up again to linger this time on the mutinous pout of her mouth.

Stung by the absolute effrontery of the hateful man, she balled her hands into fists and hissed between her teeth, 'Listen up—I'm only here with you now to make sure you don't upset Andreas beyond his bearing. And since you were crass enough to bring up the subject of the appalling mistake I made the other evening, when I thought you were a normal, straightforward sort of guy—a guy I could—' Swallowing hard, she blanked out the word *love* that had almost slipped out, and substituted, 'Like.' Then she pushed out through teeth that were chattering with tension, 'Should anything come of my mistake, then *I'll* cope with it.' She collided with eyes that were boring into her with the intensity of a laser beneath slightly peaking brows, and shot out for good measure, 'I wouldn't marry *you* if you held a gun to my head!'

And then, unforgivably, he threw back his head and roared with laughter.

Noting the imminent approach of the prettier of

the two female cabin crew, all sultry dark eyes and come-hither smiles for Dimitri, Bonnie jerked her head round and stared fixedly out of the window to stop herself either launching at him, fists flying, or bursting into tears. Because just for a moment he'd sloughed off the coolly tough tycoon image and become the laidback, approachable man she'd fallen in love with.

She'd fallen in love with an illusion. She knew that, but it didn't make having to face the reality any less painful.

'Eat.'

'What?'

OK, so she was snapping. She couldn't help that. Blinking the moisture from her eyes, she turned again, unimpressed by the array of fine china dishes that had appeared on the table in front of her chair.

'Sorry—not hungry.'

The food looked good enough for a five-star restaurant, but she knew it would choke her—and watching him spear a huge prawn, dripping with a delicious-looking sauce, made her stomach lurch. Or maybe that tingling, rolling sensation was simply down to looking at him, to the sheer male impact of him, and remembering, reliving, how it had been when he'd made love to her.

Wimp! she grouched at herself. She'd made a bad mistake, but that was no reason to get all tearful and soppy over it. Pick yourself up, dust yourself down and get on with your life, she told herself, straining for a conviction that seemed aggravatingly just beyond her grasp—though she was sure she'd get there, given time.

And if there were consequences—something that hadn't entered her head until he'd come over all dictatorial about the possibility—then she would face them on her own. She would neither expect nor accept any help from him. As soon as the meeting with Andreas was over she'd be out of his life. Permanently.

And as for the way he'd jumped to the conclusion that she would go for a termination—well, that was an insult too far. From now on she would treat him as if he were a stranger—a slightly unpleasant one. With cool detachment and a dignified politeness. And she would ask him to explain something that had been bugging her.

The thought being father to the deed, she picked up a fork and dipped it into her bowl of salad. 'I'm surprised, but relieved that you've actually decided to see your father. However, I don't understand why you should want *me* to tag along.'

Pleased with the chilly tone she'd achieved, she examined the slice of tomato she'd captured with her fork, then laid the implement straight back down again as he casually remarked, 'Initially I thought you had something going with Papadiamantis—that you'd agreed to find me and use your undeniable powers of persuasion to entice my future business plans out of me. But, for reasons I'm sure even you would understand, I had to do a swift revision.' His attention was fixed unwaveringly on her rapidly heating face. 'Your response to me was everything a man could dream of, and more. But you were a virgin. You were no sexually promiscuous latter-day Mata Hari.'

He was even nastier than she had come to believe!

During all the time he had been promising to do what he could to locate the man she'd been seeking—*he* being that very man!—he'd believed her to be a sexual opportunist, acting on behalf of his father with whom, according to his warped mind, she was intimately involved. She was so furious the blistering words she owed him simply wouldn't formulate in her brain and then exit coherently and cuttingly from her mouth.

'I need to know what your relationship with my father is.'

'Nurse and patient!' Bonnie spat out. And then her breath solidified in her throat, preventing her from berating him for the sewer-like qualities of his mind.

He was mopping the residue of sauce from his plate with a chunk of crusty bread, and he said, as if she hadn't uttered a word, 'And I need to know what his motives for wanting to contact me after all these years really are.' His burnished eyes held contact with hers. 'Call me a cynic, but I find it difficult to believe in a road-to-Damascus conversion.'

He was obviously referring to the message she'd delivered, stating that Andreas wished to heal the breach of years and apologise for what he now admitted was his harsh treatment of his sons.

She subsided miserably in her seat. It was hopeless. She felt so sorry for his frail old father. He'd admitted his failings as a parent, was genuinely contrite. But his remaining son insisted on clinging to the resentment of a fourteen-year-old—even to the extent of working hard towards completely ruining his own father. His suspicious, cynical mind would allow no forgiveness.

Coffee was brought; plates cleared. The untouched state of Bonnie's food earned her what she could only describe as a pitying smirk from the sassy stewardess, who probably thought she was the tycoon's latest mistress in a sulk.

Bonnie didn't care *what* she thought! She took a mouthful of hot coffee, collected herself. 'If that's your attitude—if your mind is that closed—there's no point in meeting your father. No point in dragging me along. I do have a life of my own—things to do.'

Dimitri hid a smile. He could understand her anger perfectly. As far as she was concerned he had behaved abominably. Explanations were needed, and reassurances, but the time was not yet right. Not until the interview with his parent was over.

'Like getting together with your phantom fiancé?' he slid in smoothly, angling around to watch the play of emotions on her lovely face.

'There is nothing of the phantom about Troy!' Bonnie claimed rapidly, and the frown that had marred her smooth brow disappeared at the speed of light as she saw a way to put paid to his horrible threat to keep her within his sights until he discovered whether or not she was pregnant. If he thought she was in love with Troy, had promised to marry *him*, was close to him and on the brink of getting a whole lot closer, he would withdraw that threat.

Dimitri Kyriakis's pride would be of the ultra-stiff variety. He wouldn't allow himself to be second-best to any man alive.

'There was nothing unreal about the way we kissed each other while we were waiting to board the ferry! I know you saw us!' She almost added, *So there!* but thought better of it.

She bit down on her lower lip as he came back, sounding amused, 'I *know* you know I saw you. And I know it meant nothing. It told me only that you were crazy enough to think it might.' He smiled with dangerous softness. 'The vigorous punch you threw at me when you learned who I really was told me everything.'

Crazy! He was calling *her* crazy? 'I don't know what you think you're talking about,' she told him from her high horse, itching to deliver another, far more vigorous punch, but at the same time doing her best to stay calm—because if she betrayed any strong emotion where he was concerned it would give him the upper hand.

'No?' One ebony brow elevated.

His sudden smile made her heart turn over. She couldn't really believe someone so achingly good to look at could be all bad—could she? But his next words blotted out that tiny doubt as if it had never been.

'When he left you at Heathrow there were no fond farewells. In fact, I'm told he looked as if he'd just learned his numbers had come up but he'd lost his lottery ticket.'

Stunned by the implication of that information, Bonnie could only gape. Then her mouth firmed and she blurted at full pelt, 'You had us followed!'

'Stavros is good. The best. If he weren't he wouldn't be in my employ.' Dimitri shrugged his impressive shoulders just slightly, as if such underhand behaviour were nothing noteworthy, then extracted some papers from his briefcase and began to read, making several written alterations in the margins.

Bonnie closed her eyes. There was nothing else to say that would be of any use against this tricky devil. By the time she and Troy had landed at Heathrow, both travel-weary and out of sorts for different reasons, she had at last managed to convince him that there was no future for them together. And, yes, the atmosphere as they had parted to go their separate ways had been frigid, to say the least.

Bonnie dragged a comb through her hair, her eyes watering as she met the resistance of tangles, then scraped it back and anchored the blonde mass with a battery of pins.

Wearing the old-fashioned pale blue shirtwaister she'd dug out of the depths of her wardrobe back home, she looked as no-nonsense as she could manage without the armour of her work uniform—the starchy white button-through dress and flat white shoes that in her opinion made her feet look like those of a giant Minnie Mouse.

They'd spent the night at Dimitri's Athens apartment. Not giving the minimalist decor—polished blond wood, leather and teak—more than a passing glance she'd frigidly demanded to be shown to the room she was to use, thanked him with icy politeness and locked the door. And had slept barely a wink.

Now she could hear movements, smell the aroma of freshly brewed coffee, and had to steel herself to march out of her room and face him—face what the day would bring, and bolster her nerve by reminding herself that once the visit to Andreas was over she would demand to be put on a plane back to England. She picked up the overnight bag she'd packed with an immediate return journey in mind, and left the room.

Opening doors, she found him in the kitchen—a functional room of brushed steel, white-tiled walls and a table topped by black marble bearing a cafetière, earthenware mugs, a pot of honey and a bowl of fruit. It struck her that on the occasions when he had to use this place he would eat out at some fancy restaurant. The room had the atmosphere of a kitchen where no meal had ever been cooked. No family had ever gathered around that table to eat, to discuss the day's happenings, laugh together. Remembering the way *her* family, all six of them, had always gathered in the large, warm, cluttered kitchen at home to share an evening meal, she suddenly felt sorry for Dimitri. Though she reminded herself sternly he had no right to anyone's compassion, least of all hers.

She tried not to look at him, but Dimitri, turning from loading a plate with crusty rolls, looked spectacularly stunning. She had to unwillingly admit that. Wearing a beautifully tailored light grey silk business suit, that drew subtle attention to the width of his shoulders, narrow hips and long legs, and a darker grey shirt and charcoal tie, he was formidably elegant, she thought dizzily as her throat closed up.

He was a danger to the female of the species; touch him at your peril.

'You slept well?' Dark, fathomless eyes took inventory of her appearance, sweeping down from the uncompromising submission of her hair by what now felt to her like a couple of pounds of ironmongery, to the frumpy, no-nonsense statement of her ancient shirtwaister. For a moment Bonnie thought he smiled, but it was so fleeting she couldn't be sure. And his beautiful mouth was now so severe she decided that he hadn't *really* gained a nano-second's amusement from the way she was presenting herself.

'Very well, thank you,' she lied, watching, fascinated, the movement of his hands as he poured coffee for them both. Deploring the way her mind wandered off track, she wished she didn't find him so mesmerising and attractive, and swiftly reminded herself what a monster he was. Deep within that well-shaped skull was a mind that was cruel and devious. She had to remember that. Had to keep her anger at the way he had hoodwinked and used her at boiling point. It was her only defence against her disobedient body's seemingly automatic response to him.

At an autocratic gesture of one of his strong, long-fingered hands, she pulled out a steel and black leather stool and sat.

Cradling her mug in both hands to stop their annoying tremor, she took tentative sips of the hot brew. She noted that, like her, he wasn't eating, and wondered if the thought of the upcoming meeting was making him feel uncomfortable—penitent, perhaps, for the way he'd treated his father, flesh of his flesh, like a hated business enemy for so many long years. In Greece family bonds went deep, she knew that, and perhaps even he couldn't deny that inescapable pull of blood?

But when he snapped out, 'We'll go, if you're ready,' harsh lines bracketing his severely beautiful mouth, she changed her mind. He didn't have a sensitive bone in his body. Winning was the name of his game. Winning at all costs.

Dimitri drove through the frantic Athens traffic as he did everything else: as if he owned the place. Marvelling that her knuckles weren't white, Bonnie had to concede that she felt perfectly safe, and only when they had left the city behind and were heading into the hills did she shift uncomfortably in the passenger seat.

Neither of them had spoken a word since they'd left his apartment in the newly gentrified part of the old city. He hadn't even commented on the overnight bag at her feet. But what was there to say?

For her part, her thoughts centred on the despicable way he'd treated her, and his callous, unforgiving behaviour towards his father. No way was she prepared to delve into those muddy waters again. A dignified silence was best.

And as for Dimitri—a swift glance at his classically moulded profile, the tough set of his jaw and the hard line of his mouth, told her that he was lost in his own thoughts. And they weren't pleasant.

As they reached the imposing villa where she'd spent so many professionally satisfying weeks caring for Andreas Papadiamantis, the ornate electronically operated gates swung smoothly open. One of the groundsmen must have been alerted to watch for their approach, she decided, and because she just couldn't help it she twisted round in her seat and pleaded, 'Please try to reach some understanding with your father.'

'That matters to you? You are fond of him?' No

inflexion in his tone. He'd slowed the vehicle down, almost as if he wanted to defer the meeting for as long as possible.

'He was one of my easier cases,' she assured him, aware that in her renewed agitation she was babbling. 'Really brave. He knew his cancer could return, and was determined that it shouldn't. Towards the end of my time with him he told me that he wanted to keep well—buy enough time to contact you and try to put things right between you. So, yes, I suppose you could say I *am* fond of him.'

Which admission gained her nothing but cool silence. If he was mulling over what she'd said, he gave no sign of it, and Bonnie had never felt so thankful to see another human being when they drew to a halt before the flight of steps that led to the main door and Maria, Andreas's housekeeper, greeted them.

She flung her sturdy arms around Bonnie, giving her a warm hug and a cheerful, 'It's *so* good to see you again.' She turned to the watching, cold-eyed Dimitri. 'The master is waiting for you in his study. But first I should offer you coffee.'

'Thank you, no. If you will show me the way?'

Maria nodded, the chilly atmosphere making her mouth turn down at the corners before she turned and led the way into the cool interior of the villa.

Bonnie managed to tag along for all of three paces until Dimitri swung round, his arrogant head high, his black eyes cold. 'Stay. No doubt you will see your former patient later. For the moment this is a private matter.'

Disconsolately, Bonnie watched his imposing figure as he followed the housekeeper. For a moment her instinct had been to defy him, to march right into the study behind him. But only for a moment. She wouldn't put it past Dimitri Kyriakis to bodily throw her out, and that would only add to the tension of the meeting between father and son.

Wandering through the villa, she gained the pool area and sat beneath the shade of one of the brightly coloured parasols to watch the water.

She felt such a failure. Andreas had been so keen to have her sit in on the meeting, but Dimitri had made sure that she wouldn't be around to pour oil on possibly turbulent waters. All she could do was sit and wait, and hope for a positive outcome.

And it was stupid of her to wish she'd never set eyes on either of them, because between them they'd managed to create turmoil in her hitherto unruffled life.

She couldn't put the clock back, no matter how hard she wished she could.

What seemed like hours later, Bonnie heard approaching footsteps and her shoulders tightened with added tension, to relax just a little when Andreas exclaimed, 'I thought we would find you here. It was always your favourite place in your off-duty hours!'

He sounded fairly cheerful. And that had to be a good sign. Scrambling to her feet, Bonnie noted that although he was smiling his eyes looked red-rimmed. She shot an accusing glance at Dimitri, shattered by the treacherous sensation that shot through her as she looked into his lean, strong features. She hated herself for her unwanted physical response to him more than she hated him for the evidence that he had reduced this frail old man to tears.

He had hurt her, made her look the biggest fool alive, and yet he still had the power to make her heart turn over, raise goosebumps on her skin when she remembered—

Fighting to consign those memories to the dustbin of really bad mistakes, she gave all her attention to Andreas. Wearing a pristine white linen suit, he looked wonderfully relaxed—so whatever had passed between him and his son couldn't have been all bad.

She'd probably never know, she conceded as the elderly man placed his hands on her shoulders and kissed her cheek, murmuring, 'Thank you,' and then saying more strongly, 'We will take a glass of wine together, and Maria will serve us lunch.'

Bonnie gave a huge smile. Mission accomplished! Father and son under the same roof, sharing a meal. A giant step in the right direction.

Only to have her optimism flattened as Dimitri put in, coolly polite, 'Thank you, but I'm afraid we will have to pass. Bonnie and I have some business to attend to.'

'What business?' Bonnie demanded, as soon as she'd fastened her seat belt, having been hustled from the villa at what she considered indecent haste.

Giving her an unreadable look before firing the ignition, Dimitri imparted, 'My father tells me he has asked you to marry him. Can that be true?'

CHAPTER TEN

IGNORING the question as being completely irrelevant—and none of his business, in any case—Bonnie gave full rein to the matter she knew was far more important. She employed the crisp tone she kept for recalcitrant patients.

'Would it have hurt you to stay for lunch? Or if you couldn't manage that you could have at least spared another half an hour and taken a glass of wine with your father. Andreas looked dreadfully disappointed,' she wound up, on a note of disapproval.

'Because I whisked his bride-to-be away?'

Hating his scathing tone, the way he seemed to ignore any criticism and turn it back on *her*, she snapped, 'Don't be so silly!'

Noting the way his mouth twitched at one corner, she took a deep breath and struggled for a more conciliatory tone, 'Anyway, how did it go? Did the two of you reach an understanding, at least? Will you be seeing your father again?'

She had invested a lot of time and trouble, not to mention suffering the fall-out from her own volcanic relationship with Dimitri, trying to bring about a reconciliation between the two men. She was itching to know what had happened, but had the feeling he wouldn't tell her.

She was right. He didn't.

A private matter, he'd said. And he was keeping it that way. They had negotiated the gates and were back on the open road. Bonnie sank back in her seat, folding her arms across her midriff, her soft mouth set. It didn't matter. He could keep his mouth zipped. As soon as she was back in England she would phone Andreas and *he* would put her in the picture— after all, he had wanted her to sit in on the tricky first meeting, but Dimitri had squashed any hope of that. Her natural curiosity would have to wait a little longer to be satisfied.

'I asked you a question. Did you accept his proposal? Or did you string him along on the off-chance that a better offer might pop up on the horizon?' He sounded grim. *Looked* grim, she noted, flicking a look at his set profile. He was driving far too fast for the condition of the narrow winding road.

Could he be jealous? He sounded jealous. She took the thought and examined it, and immediately discarded it. Of *course* he wasn't jealous! Women like her were two a penny as far as he was concerned. He'd only made love to her because he could; she was there, she was willing. He'd said he'd marry her if she was carrying his child. From some archaic sense of duty, no doubt.

Deciding that he might slow down if she stopped annoying him and answered his question, she widened her grey eyes at an approaching hairpin bend and stated rapidly, 'I am not, as you so quaintly put it, your father's "bride-to-be".' She held her breath as he successfully negotiated the scary bend, then rushed on, 'He *did* ask me to marry him, but only because he'd come to rely on me. It often happens— a patient's fixation on his nurse. It wears off as soon as life returns to normal. Naturally I said no. Why would I want to be married in name only to an old man? Though naturally I didn't put it like that,' she assured him in haste. 'I like to believe I was a bit more diplomatic in my refusal.'

'So no mention, in my father's case, of a gun to the head?'

She heard the dry thread of amusement in his voice and marvelled at his sudden change of attitude. She sensed the way he took his attention from the road and turned to look at her, and wished he wouldn't—the road demanded all his attention and driving skills.

Then she felt her toes curling in her shoes as he added, his voice thick with meaning, 'I can't imagine any man having the strength of will to leave his marriage to *you* unconsummated. It would be more than flesh and blood could stand. Taking you to bed would be top of the list of any man's priorities.'

In spite of actively despising him for the type of man he was, Bonnie could no more deny the hot stab of naked desire that snaked right through her entire body than she could jump through the roof of the car and fly. It was humiliating to have to admit that, in spite of knowing how duplicitous he was, it didn't alter his incredible physical appeal. It should do, but it didn't.

To bolster her sagging self-defence mechanisms, she told him prissily, 'Keep your eyes on the road or we'll end up in a ditch—or worse. And anyway—' her eyes narrowed suspiciously '—where are we going?'

This wasn't the road that would take them back into the city. She'd borrowed one of Andreas's cars on a couple of occasions, and driven to Athens to pick up personal bits and bobs while she'd been caring for him, so she knew it wasn't.

'To my main home in Greece. I only use the Athens apartment when I'm locked into back-to-back meetings that span a few days.'

Her tummy clenched, and a tiny shiver rippled down her spine. He might be planning to drop by his home to give her lunch before driving her back to the airport. But she didn't think so.

Testing the water, she announced, 'I need to be at the airport as soon as possible to wait until I can get a flight to England. So I'll have to pass on the home visit.'

She received what she'd fully dreaded and half

expected. 'Apparently you're not due to report for duty for around a fortnight. Molly has the impression you'll take the opportunity of seeing more of my country.'

So he and her mother had got cosy, on first-name terms, while she'd been packing for what she'd reckoned would be a forty-eight-hour stay away!

'You won't be returning to England until I know whether or not you are carrying my child. And even then maybe not. Wedding invitations can be delivered by phone.'

Seriously rattled, Bonnie screeched, 'You can't be serious!' uncaring that she sounded like a bad tempered child. 'It's kidnap! I'll report you to the police if you don't let me out of this car right now!'

'And what would you do, stranded in the middle of nowhere?' he delivered in a tone of sweetness and light. 'Calm down, Bonnie, and look at the situation logically. Pregnant or not, I want you as my wife. And that's something I've never said to any woman. Something, in fact, I've avoided like the plague. So look on the next week or two as an opportunity for us to get to know each other thoroughly.'

Stunned, Bonnie could only gape at him, unaware that he'd pulled the car to a halt in front of a low stone building. Aware only that he'd turned to her, one arm sliding behind her on the back of the passenger seat, lush lashes veiling his eyes, his smile sensual and soft.

Almost idly he lifted a hand and brushed the

stray strand of hair that had escaped from her armoury of pins back from her overheated forehead. Her mouth trembled at the light drift of his touch, and the pure temptation of his mouth magnetised her gaze—the fizzing battery of sensations were doing her no good at all!

To stamp down on her body's treacherous reaction to him she growled, 'Don't touch me!' all the time knowing his touch was what she craved most in the world.

He ignored her protestation as if it were unworthy of a moment's consideration, his hand slipping to the back of her head and deftly removing the pins until the shimmering mass of her hair tumbled to her shoulders. 'I prefer your hair loose. So humour me, hmm?'

The fingers of his hand gently caressed the tender nape of her neck and her heart stopped. She couldn't breathe, and almost cried out with the sense of loss when he withdrew his hand, turned and slid his long legs out of the car.

Shame at her weakness engulfed her in a bitter tide, and in only the time it took him to walk round the front of the car and open the door at her side she got herself back on track—partially, at least. Right now it looked as if she was stuck here with him. She had to use the time to convince him that, fancy the pants off him as she might, no way could she marry him. What sane woman could hope for lasting happiness with a man who was as devious as a cartload of monkeys? A man who was mean-minded enough to hold a grudge over something that had happened decades ago, and set out cold-bloodedly to ruin his own father?

She exited the car, brushing aside his helping hand. Touching was out. She couldn't trust herself.

One eyebrow rose at the way her gorgeous little nose was pointing skywards. His smile slight and quirky, he reached into the well of the car and lifted her bag. 'Welcome to my home, Bonnie.'

It nestled in a green hollow, with a backdrop of silver olive trees, a haze of tall scrub, and the punctuation marks of tall dark green cypresses. The stones of the building had been colour-washed in pale ochre, a shade echoed by the ancient roof tiles, and the window shutters were a deep faded blue. Bonnie, stepping onto a path set with a mosaic of small rounded stones bordered by aromatic rosemary and colourful marigolds, blurted, 'It's really homey!'

'Don't sound so surprised.' He was stepping onto the stone slabs that formed a narrow terrace in front of the property and he turned, tilting his dark head as he spoke.

Bonnie, meeting the slightly amused query in his eyes, assessing the impressive height of him, the exclusive, commanding maleness of him, the way the immaculately tailored grey silk suit drew discreet attention to the width of his shoulders, the narrowness of his hips and the length of long

powerful legs, could only say, in all honesty, 'I
would have thought you'd be far more at home in
something palatial, with an army of servants bowing
and scraping at every corner.'

'Ah.' His eyes crinkled at the corners. 'Then that
shows you know very little about me.' He placed a
hand on the small of her back, ushering her over the
threshold into a long low room, paved in the dusky
pink of antique terracotta tiles and dotted with softening rugs of deep umber and cream geometric
designs. There was a stone fireplace at either end,
around which were grouped two-seater sofas covered in beige linen, and the centre of the room was
taken up by a pale ash wood table upon which sat a
bowl of vibrant marigolds.

'I will show you the rest of my home later. But
first a cold drink. Please make yourself comfortable.'

Unwillingly, but for the moment seeing no other
option, Bonnie took a corner of one of the sofas,
feeling like Alice in Wonderland. Her eyes wide, she
took in the shafts of sunlight as they poured through
small windows set into the thick stone walls as
Dimitri exited through a narrow doorway which she
supposed led to a kitchen.

She'd spoken the truth when she'd said that she
wouldn't have put him in this attractive but humbly
rustic setting in a million years. It was the sort of
place an ordinary working girl like her, a working
girl with romantic notions of rural Greece, would

choose if she had the chance. Not the choice of permanent home for a hard-nosed and—let's face it— hard-hearted businessman.

The cold drink, when it arrived, turned out to be champagne. Dimitri had shed his suit jacket, and the sleeves of his darker grey shirt were rolled up, exposing the hair-roughened olive-toned skin of his firmly muscled forearms. Bonnie looked away quickly, fruitlessly wishing he didn't have the power to make her breath become erratic and her heart beat like a crazy thing. He didn't have to do or say anything. He only had to be there, she decided mournfully.

He poured the foaming liquid into two plain but elegant flutes, placed the bottle on a hitherto unnoticed low table at her side, and told her, 'Anna—who comes in most days to look after the house for me—has left us cold chicken for lunch. I hope you are hungry. She is deeply insulted if there are any leftovers.'

Handing her a flute, he sank into the opposite end of the sofa, his long legs angled towards her, his knees touching the skirts of her dowdy dress. Feeling awkward, and plain ridiculous, Bonnie wondered what she was doing here. Sitting around, letting him ply her with liquor, when if she'd had any backbone and her brain had been working she should already be stumping along that dusty road, calling on Andreas and begging him to ask one of his staff to drive her to the airport. It couldn't be more than eight or nine miles, and she could manage that. She was no size zero weakling.

And then his next words reminded her that she really did have a sensible reason for hanging around—just for a little while.

'Will you be happy here? If not, we have the choice of a house in Paris or a penthouse apartment in London, all fully staffed and kept for when I need to visit on business. It is entirely your decision. I will be happy wherever you are, *pethi mou*.'

Whatever that meant! She supposed it was an endearment. She wanted to slap it back down his throat! Appalled by the violence he goaded her into, she swallowed a gulp of champagne to stifle her need to shriek at him—because he had to be winding her up. She put her glass down on the little table with a decisive click and told him, as composed as she could be under the circumstances, 'As I won't be marrying you, baby or no baby, the question of whether or not I could be happy here or in any other of your swanky pads doesn't arise.'

'You may think that now, but I will change your mind.'

Arrogance personified!

Yet she knew, to her shame, that he only had to reach for her, take her in his arms and kiss her, and she wouldn't have any mind worth the name left to resist him. She lifted her fingertips to her pounding temples, realised her hands were shaking, and hated herself for being so hopeless.

Determined to do something about that state of affairs, behave like a grown-up, she screwed herself further into the sofa, ignoring the knowing twist of his sensational mouth, and told him firmly, 'Let's be sensible about the situation.'

Her eyes were now fixed firmly on her hands—which, in her lap, were twisting together, reflecting the inner agitation she didn't want him to detect in her voice. She didn't dare look at him. One glance at that lean, devastatingly handsome face and she became a victim of raging hormones, and she couldn't afford that.

'I can do sensible.'

Bonnie tightened her lips. That was news to her. His behaviour to date had been anything *but* sensible. 'Fine. Then you'll see that all this talk of marriage is totally off the wall? We made a mistake. A Greek island, a romantic setting, wine, moonlight—mistakes were made. It happens.'

'But never before to you?'

She gulped. She refused to let him deflect her. So he'd been her first lover? He didn't need to think that gave him any leverage. 'Beside the point. The point is,' she stressed, 'because of one mistake you don't have to get it in your head that marriage is the only way out. Why make such a sacrifice?'

'It would be no sacrifice,' he drawled, his accent thick.

Ignoring that interruption, and the shiver down her taut spine his words had provoked, Bonnie soldiered on. 'If I'm pregnant—which I doubt—then I'll cope on my own. The bare minimum of maintenance would be accepted, if offered—I'm not some greedy harpy, but neither am I too proud to take a small amount of financial assistance towards the upkeep of your child. If there is one. Should you want visiting rights, I wouldn't make any objection. I am capable of civilised behaviour.'

Suddenly the thought of having a child of his— dark hair, jet-black eyes and smooth golden limbs, a child she would love to pieces—turned her heart to mush and brought a teary, emotional lump to her throat.

It seriously disadvantaged her, and his softly inserted, 'Would marriage to me be such a terrible sacrifice, Bonnie?' showed he hadn't given a single thing she'd said any consideration whatsoever. It was the final straw.

Her smoky grey eyes darkening with angry frustration, she collided with the dark warmth of his unwavering gaze and spluttered, 'Tell me why I would agree to marry a man who thinks so badly of me? You admitted it! First, without knowing a single thing about me, you decided I use sex to get what I want, as some sort of a spy sent by your father to find you and seduce you into spilling your latest miserable business plans. Then you decide you got it wrong.' Her face flamed as she remembered exactly what had happened to make him revise that sleazy opinion. 'So you pin another nasty label on me—I'm a gold-digger, the sort of woman who would half promise to marry an old man while keeping her eye open for a better prospect! Why would you want to tie yourself to a woman you lose no opportunity to think the very worst of—please tell me!'

Running out of steam, she just glared at him, her hands balling into fists. She was unprepared for his admission.

'I made a serious error of judgement for the first time in my life, I am ashamed to say. Based at first on cynicism and then on pure emotion. Jealousy. I have never had occasion to suffer that unpleasant affliction before, believe me! That weakness made me angry enough to accuse you of being something I know full well you're not.'

A dull flush of colour touched his superb cheekbones and he spread his hands in a gesture that admitted failure.

'You've made no secret of your fondness for your former patient—you even went to the trouble of hunting me down on his behalf. And when he told me how much he admired you, said he'd proposed to you, I wanted to strangle him!'

Unimpressed, Bonnie shrugged her slender shoulders. That outburst had told her that the grudge that had driven him for all his adult life was far from forgotten.

She had no idea how the subject of Andreas's proposal had come up, but she could imagine the older man's self-deprecating shrug, the wry smile aimed against himself when he'd offered that information. And she could just see Dimitri's face when he'd learned that the father he'd set out to destroy actually wanted to marry the woman who might be carrying *his* child! Like a feral dog standing guard over a bone!

He might be stunning to look at, but his character needed a drastic makeover!

He leaned forward and took both her hands in his. Bonnie tried to pull them away, but his grip only tightened. 'We were good together,' he said in a hoarse undertone. 'I knew we would be.'

Fruitlessly renewing her efforts to free her hands from his, Bonnie knew her face was flaming. He was such a cad! Would he *never* let her forget the worst mistake she'd ever made?

'When I first saw your photograph I thought you were the most beddable woman I'd ever set eyes on. I was hooked and didn't know it.'

'What photograph?' Bonnie's hands stilled within his grasp. This conversation was getting seriously weird. 'I don't know what you're talking about.'

'Of course you don't. Come here.' He released her hands, slid an arm behind her waist and tugged her against his side. 'A while ago, my enemy—Andreas— disappeared off the radar. While I have always shunned press intrusion, my father had always seemed to court it. Then, for three months, nothing. I now know that he wanted to keep news of his possibly fatal illness, his operation, out of the public domain, fearing a loss of confidence in his last remaining business interests.

'However, at the time I was unaware of all that. I was curious, needing to know what the old devil was up to. The private investigator I hired managed to get close enough to penetrate the villa's security and take photographs of a beautiful blonde lazing by the pool. Now, this I *did* know about my father: he'd had two wives but never a fully paid-up mistress. Any extra-marital activities he might have indulged in were swift, secret and probably sordid. So the installation at his villa of a luscious blonde had to mean there would soon be an announcement of a third marriage.'

Bonnie blinked. Her eyes had grown heavy. Being held so close to him, listening to his sultry, sexy voice, was putting her in a trance! Let her guard down and she was in real danger of letting him talk her into anything! Into believing she could really love the type of man she knew him to be.

Pushing her hands against his chest, she shoved, gaining enough space to allow her to fix him with a hastily manufactured glare. 'What nonsense! When your father rested in the afternoons it was my time off. Mostly I took advantage of the pool. Do you always make things up to suit your own warped agenda?'

'In your case, it seems I have done!' He took her hands, raised them to his lips, and dropped lingering kisses in the palms. Bonnie so wished he hadn't.

Alarmingly, she could feel her breasts push against the confines of her bra. It took a monumental effort to snatch her hands away, but she managed it and sat on them.

She could hear the amusement in his voice as he confessed, 'And there's worse to come. When the luscious blonde turned up, literally on my doorstep, saying she was looking for Dimitri Kyriakis I immediately thought my father had sent his woman to try and find out what my future plans were. Then you jumped to the conclusion that I was Stavros. I let that ride. Promised to find out the whereabouts of the Kyriakis villa. I knew none of the locals would give any information away about the wealthy families who make the island their private holiday retreat. They rely too much on the extra income, and fiercely guard against intruding journalists or gawpers.'

'You made a fool of me—and I'll never forgive that!' Bonnie promised, incandescent with rage. He'd made her an object of private ridicule, made her believe she'd fallen in love with him! He had to be the vilest man she'd ever encountered!

Her face scarlet, she shuffled her bottom. Sitting on her hands was proving to be decidedly uncomfortable, and probably undignified. But she was past caring and launched at full volume.

'You could have told me straight off who you were. I'd have given you your father's message and that would have been that!'

'And missed out on the fun we had, *pethi mou*? I don't think so.' He was actually grinning! And his voice wasn't quite steady—he was laughing at her! He explained, without a shadow of remorse, 'When I decided to string you along it was at the back of my mind that you might, if frustrated enough, use your seduction techniques on me to gain the information you needed. I have to admit I was looking forward to it! The signals you gave out told me you were almost as physically attracted to me as I was to you. In the end it was I who did the seducing—and earned myself quite a shock. Truly, I was going to come clean the next day. But, alas, Athena got there first.'

And then Bonnie had socked him one!

Bonnie decided to keep her hands well out of harm's way and leave them where they were, getting cramp, in case she forgot her manners again in a big way and gave a repeat performance.

And then she had the breath knocked out of her lungs when Dimitri confided, with a sincerity even her rock-bottom opinion of him couldn't deny, 'I'd meant to explain all this—why I'd behaved as I had—meant to woo you properly, tell you how much you'd come to mean to me. But enough of all that for the moment.' He was on his feet in one fluid movement. 'Let us eat and talk of other things. I will feast my eyes on your lovely face and remember the way you look when not wearing something that resembles a swamping old curtain!'

Releasing her poor hands, Bonnie rubbed them absentmindedly to get the circulation going and watched him walk through the narrow door. Could she believe him? Did she dare? She wanted to—so much her heart hurt. Given his history with his estranged father, she could understand why, on seeing photographs of her clad in a skimpy bikini, stretched out beside Andreas's opulent pool, he should have formed such a low opinion of her.

And naturally her appearance at his island hideaway, looking for him, would have aroused his suspicions. He'd known she was there at the bidding of his father, and his regrettably cynical nature would have led him to believe talk of a message was a ploy, that the real game was business espionage.

But once aware of the contents of that message he'd acted upon them. She had to be fair. And maybe he'd been telling the truth when he'd stated he'd intended to come clean the next day, woo her? But things had happened—in the shape of Athena's bombshell and the arrival of Troy.

Her brow wrinkled as she tried to pull all the pieces together. If he hadn't meant what he'd just said, why would he have had her followed? Why turn up at her home? It couldn't be down, as he'd said, to the maybe-baby, because hadn't he stated he wanted her as his wife, pregnant or not?

Bonnie chewed down on her lower lip. Could she allow her love for him to blossom? Could she trust her future happiness to a man with such deplorable character faults—namely his long-held grudge against his father?

CHAPTER ELEVEN

BEFORE they ate Dimitri insisted on giving her a tour of the property. Pride and perhaps something deeper glowed in his dark eyes as he escorted her from the main living room, and she seized on the diversion gratefully as a way of taking her mind off her muddled feelings.

The room beyond where they'd been sitting was a study, fitted out with all the latest electronic equipment. 'I do as much work as I can from home,' he explained, before showing her through to the kitchen, a welcoming place, with a huge range, chunky oak tables, dried herbs hanging from the rafters. From there they moved to a small hallway with a large window looking out onto a terrace set with a long table, surrounded by terracotta pots billowing with scarlet geraniums.

'A lovely place to sit in the evening sun, sipping wine and watching the swallows swoop to their nests in the eaves,' he told her, walking before her to the narrow twisting staircase.

Three bedrooms, with greyish silver pine floors, huge double beds, old-fashioned chests in rich, well-polished wood, and a bathroom that was the last word in modern luxury, with touches of the ancient in the colourful Cretan wall tiles. Everywhere held the atmosphere of this being a cherished home.

Now they were seated at one end of the pale ash wood table, facing each other over a platter of cold chicken, olives, cold rice salad mixed with tomatoes, strips of brilliantly coloured red and green peppers, olive oil and lemon juice. Bonnie, helping herself to healthy portions of each dish, knew she had to reach a decision. A decision that would affect the rest of her life.

But not now. Now she just wanted to keep away from anything contentious, to savour this totally relaxed atmosphere, enjoy the warmth flowing from him, enfolding her. Just for a little while. Find a subject that wouldn't raise the doubts she didn't want to have to struggle with right now.

'You have a lovely home.' She kept her eyes on her plate. Looking at him always affected her judgement, so she wouldn't. 'How did you find it?'

'It was my mother's home for the first fifteen years of her life. Times were hard. My grandparents were peasants, scratching a living. My mother had to go to the city to find work. She had no siblings. It was up to her to send money home.' He laid his cutlery down. Unlike her, he had barely touched the meal.

Glancing up, Bonnie saw the sudden emptiness

of his eyes, and believed she knew why when he told her, 'Having no son, and a wife who was by that time ailing, my grandfather apparently gave up. When I found this place it was almost derelict, my family all dead. I traced the landlord, made him an offer he couldn't refuse, and set about renovating it.'

'That's so sad,' Bonnie sympathised. 'Did you know your grandparents?'

'They died before I was born. And now we talk of happier things.'

His smile gleamed, but it didn't reach his eyes, and as he told her how he'd hunted down suitable furniture—the ornately carved bed in the master bedroom had been found in a Paris junk shop, restored and shipped over—Bonnie decided she knew what grieved him.

He'd talked of the lost family on his mother's side. All these years on he was extremely wealthy, but his wealth had come far too late to help the grandparents he'd never known, had obviously heard of from his mother.

But at least his mother had had a reversal of fortune—meeting and marrying a business tycoon, Andreas Papadiamantis. Had Andreas refused to offer financial help to his peasant in-laws? Was that what had caused the rift between father and son? Was it enough to make the son carry a grudge that had lasted all his adult life?

But Dimitri had never actually *known* his grandparents. So surely that couldn't be a strong enough motive for what had turned out to be a single-minded ruthless determination to bring his father's business empire to ruin? It was an enigma without a solution. Unless she asked him outright.

Later...

Andreas had told her his first wife had died. Dimitri's mother had to have been that wife. He'd also said that his firstborn son had died of drug overdose. Unsure of the chronology of events, she hazarded, 'You must have been gutted when both your mother *and* your brother died.'

She was totally unprepared for his reaction, for his harsh, 'You ask too many questions.'

The sense of rejection swamped her, sent a chill rippling down her spine. He looked so closed, so distant.

'You make me feel such an outsider. You say you want to marry me, but you shut me out of what's obviously important to you.'

'Don't open Pandora's box. You may not like what you find,' he advised coolly, rising to his feet and collecting her overnight bag from where it had been left inside the main door. He extended a hand to her. 'Come, choose which room you would like to use. And then I will show you my orange grove, and the stream which tumbles out of the rocks on the far hillside. And we have a swimming pool—part natural rock, part manmade. Then maybe we will talk of the future for a change, *ne*?'

If they had a future together. Part of her wanted

it with a ferocity that frightened her, pushing her towards the unknown. Yet another part urged extreme caution.

He'd said he wanted her as his wife, wanted her in his bed. Yet he'd never mentioned the L word, never once said he loved her, and there was a part of his life that was not to be spoken of, not to be questioned.

She looked at his outstretched hand. So much was at stake here. She really did need more time to discover him, the real Dimitri Kyriakis, what made him tick, made him the man he was. Sexy as sin, a devastating charmer when he wanted to be, a man who held grudges, held secrets.

Besides, he was offering to allow her to choose her own room, which meant he didn't intend them to sleep together. That was a huge plus, because she was fully aware of her limitations where he was concerned. If he so much as touched her, her thinking processes went walkabout.

She took his hand.

Mistake. As his strong fingers closed around hers everything inside her melted. Hunger for him made her breath tremble in her throat. She wanted to trust him, to rejoice in her love for him, so badly that tears sprang to her eyes. On legs that felt unsteady, she allowed him to lead her from the room.

Five minutes later, grabbing back control of her senses, she said, not quite steadily, '*This* room's lovely,' and made herself concentrate on that. It was cool, painted white, the cover on the huge bed a lovely shade of blue, matching the shutters and the lapis lazuli of the sky.

Her eyes misted all over again. She could be so happy here with him. But how long would that happiness last? How long would it be before the cracks began to show? How long before her uncertainty and his secrecy created an unbridgeable gap between them?

As if sensing her mood, he dropped her bag on the floor and caught her to him. 'Everything will be all right, Bonnie. I promise. You must trust me to make you happy. Nothing else matters.'

With his hand holding her bright head against his shoulder, she felt as if she had come home. As her own hands splayed against the breadth of his muscular chest she could feel every beat of his heart, feel the warmth of him, the increased pace of his breathing.

She wanted him so badly she didn't know what to do with herself. It was with a sense of fatalism that she felt her breasts tingle, the crests tighten and sensitise, and she knew she had to know again the glorious ecstasy that had changed her world on the night he had made love to her that first time.

'Ah, Bonnie—' His voice shook a little as he spoke her name, and she lifted her head, her eyes rising to his, meeting the slumbrous desire in the dark depths that were partly screened by thick, lush lashes. She knew she had no defences against him, and to prove it her lips parted without any instruction from her, to receive the first of a battery of tiny, teasing, tormenting kisses.

Tormenting… Tense anticipation was rippling down the length of her spine and she was unashamedly clinging now, the blood in her veins turning to fire as his body hardened against the soft swell of her tummy, his strong thighs easing her backwards, strong arms raising her, his sensual mouth trailing down her throat before he lowered her to the bed.

Leaning over her, he let his long fingers deftly and tenderly arrange the silky mass of her hair into a pale gleaming fan against the pillows, finally stroking over her cheekbones to the corners of her mouth. 'You are so beautiful, my Bonnie.' His slow smile turned her heart over. 'I think I am in heaven.'

Heaven. The touch of his hands was more than heaven as he slid the buttons of her dress from their moorings, parted the fabric to lay her throbbing body, clad in bra and briefs, unshielded from his spectacular eyes.

The front fastening of her bra was swiftly dealt with, exposing the straining mounds, and she heard him murmur in a roughened undertone, *'Theos—'* before he enclosed one engorged pink nipple and then the other with his lips. She gasped as electrified response shot down to the slick, hot heart of her femininity.

Her arms snaked up to hold him to her, and she knew she was squirming, in blatant invitation, and she could do nothing about it. Didn't want to. The raw power of what he and he alone could do to her was too strong to resist.

'Patience.' He took her wrists, lowered her arms and stood upright, unbuttoning his shirt, shrugging out of it to reveal his magnificent torso, sleek olive-toned skin roughened by dark body hair that arrowed down to the narrow waistband of his trousers.

Bonnie's mouth went dry. He was so beautiful, so sensationally male—and hers if she wanted him. And she did. Oh, how she did!

'Dimitri—' But the confession of love that was bubbling up inside her, bursting for release, went unsaid as an unwelcome shrillness sullied the very air.

His brows snapped together at the persistence of the sound. Muttering something that sounded like an expletive, he fished his mobile from the back pocket of his tailored trousers, snapped it open, registered the caller, and snapped out something terse and rapid in his own language. He listened to whoever was speaking for a moment, before ending the call and switching the phone off.

'As I told my father—he has a dreadful sense of timing!' His tone was clipped but his smile was apologetic.

Bonnie wriggled up against the pillows, the fog clearing from her brain as if a blast of cool air had cleared an area of cold clarity between the occluding mists of raw passion. On the very brink of con fiding her love for him, of promising to marry him, adore him for ever, the interruption that had seemed so brutal at the time had brought her crashing back to her senses.

He had to open up to her—he *had* to! Mentally as well as physically. Physically he was fantastically open and generous, so much so he overwhelmed her, but what went on in his head was a closed book.

Dimitri tossed the offending mobile onto the low table beside the head of the bed, his hands going to his taut waist, to the band of his trousers. Bonnie, her mouth drying, said wildly, 'If we're to be together we have to trust each other more than anyone else alive.' Her huge eyes pleaded. 'No secrets!'

'I would trust you with my life, my sweet Bonnie.'

'But not with your secrets!' The breath sobbed in her lungs.

Dimitri paced forward. His smile was wry, and the way one side of his mouth dipped made her shiver with tension. He took her hands, untangled them. She hadn't realised she'd been clasping them so tightly until he raised them to his lips and grazed soft kisses over her whitened knuckles. 'What brought this on?' His powerful gaze held her more securely than a shackle.

'That phone call from your father reminded me. Oh—I'm handling this badly!' She reclaimed her hands. Physical contact was out. At least for now.

Determined to press that decision home, she scrabbled for the edges of the coverlet and wrapped them around her nakedness.

She needed to know he could trust her with everything. Without that commitment how could a marriage work?

'So it comes back to Andreas?' His face was shuttered as his shadowed eyes took in the bunchy parcel she'd made of herself.

'It *has* to,' she agreed in abject misery, willing him to understand.

'Why?' One dark brow elevated.

'Because you just clam up on the subject.'

'Why complicate matters?' He was already reaching for his discarded shirt.

Going into panic mode, Bonnie yelped out, 'Because there's a big part of your life you won't share with me! You won't even tell me how your meeting with your father went. I'm asking you to be open, to tell me why a young teenager should walk away from his home, his father, and spend practically the rest of his life in a ruthless vendetta! Don't you see?' Her face was paper-white as she pleaded. 'The thought of such a long and remorseless grudge over something that must have happened when you were little more than a child gives me the shivers. Help me to understand.'

Deaf ears wasn't in it, Bonnie thought, her rigidly held spine sagging as he shrugged into his shirt and told her, without a trace of the accent that came into prominence when he was in the grip of strong emotion, 'It doesn't matter. It has no impact on what you and I want from each other. Think about that while I walk off the unpleasant effect of frustration. I may be some time.'

CHAPTER TWELVE

How long Bonnie huddled there, wrapped in the blue coverlet, she couldn't have said. But she knew what she had to do now, she told herself, as she listlessly dressed in the washed-out shirtwaister that Dimitri had so unflatteringly likened to an old curtain.

Dimitri.

Her soft mouth tightened. She could be tough when she had to be, and from now on she wouldn't give him head room. She couldn't afford to, because she knew she would go to pieces if she did—become one of those sad creatures who wept and wailed over a lost love, lost weight, developed black rings around sorrowful eyes and became a pain to be around.

The one and only time his name would feature would be at the top of her list of 'Things To Do'.

She would demand—yes, *demand*—he take her to the airport.

She would be back in England in good time to

help her mother with the party preparations, and when the time came she would mix with the guests, chatter and laugh as if she hadn't a care in the world.

She would then report for duty and get on with her life—keep busy, busy, *busy*.

And if it turned out she was pregnant—well, she'd worry about that if it happened.

Mentally formulating her list gave her something to think about until she arrived downstairs. She had no idea how long he'd be. He'd been frustrated and coldly angry, arrogantly disgusted with her because she'd wanted answers to her questions. Nobody, but *nobody* questioned Dimitri Kyriakis' thoughts, movements or motivations!

It might take some time for him to walk off that cocktail of emotions.

She was supposed, like an unthinking bimbo, to take him on trust. Or not at all.

Her eyes stung with hot tears. Recognising the danger signs of allowing herself to think about him, she hauled herself together smartly, swallowed the lump in her throat, and bustled around clearing away the lunch things, scraping leftovers into the wastebin and sending a silent apology to the absent part-time housekeeper.

When every last dish, plate, piece of glass or cutlery had been washed in the deep stone sink and put away, Bonnie fetched her mobile from her bag and walked out onto the terrace, the hot sun scorching her skin through the cotton dress.

Contacting Andreas would give her something to do. Something positive. She had grown fond of the old man, pitied him. And she *had* been the one to facilitate the hoped-for meeting with his son. She had every right to know how that meeting had gone, and Dimitri had flatly refused to tell her.

She could do her best to console the old man if things had gone badly—which in view of Dimitri's silence on the subject was highly possible. After all, a man who'd carried such a single-minded grudge for all those years was hardly likely to forget it just like that, to apologise, kiss and make up, was he?

Pushing out her full lower lip, she huffed at the annoying strand of hair that was getting in her eyes and set off through the grounds to find some secluded place to make her phone call.

Dimitri would blow his top if he returned to find her deep in conversation with his father. Whatever had happened was a private matter, in his set-in-stone opinion, and he would be incensed by what he would see as her meddling—with some justification, she had to admit.

Passing bee-busy flowerbeds and a huge vegetable patch, with a sprinkler going full blast, she saw an elderly man hoeing between the rows of tomato plants. He gave her a gappy grin as she approached. His trousers were tied up with string. She wondered if he was any relation to the housekeeper.

Raising her hand in response, trying to smile but she feared failing dismally, she cut off down a path that led to the orange grove Dimitri had mentioned, glad of the dappled shade. Finally going through a gap in an evergreen hedge, she came upon the pool.

A natural basin in the rock, scooped out over aeons by the action of the fall of spring water, had been sensitively extended with dark moss-green marble. The overflow meandered, fern-bordered, into a shallow ravine, where it gurgled and chattered over a stony bed and on into the valley beyond.

It must have been quite some feat of engineering, so seamlessly marrying the manmade with the natural, Bonnie marvelled as she sank down gratefully on the mossy bank, peering into the depths, meeting her reflection on the untroubled surface. But whatever Dimitri Kyriakis did he did very well. Like keeping secrets from the woman he said he wanted to marry!

Rapidly dismissing him from her mind, wishing he didn't have the knack of invading her thoughts when she least expected it, she concentrated on her reflection. Her hair, as usual, was all over the place, and there was a frown line between her eyes. She hadn't realised she was frowning. Was it to become permanent? The outward, involuntary sign of a woman disappointed in love?

Sighing, she flipped open her phone and clicked on Andreas's number, biting her lips at the length of time it took for his housekeeper to find him.

At last. 'Bonnie—how good to hear you! Is my son with you?'

'Not at the moment.' She couldn't tell him Dimitri was somewhere out there, walking off bad temper and sexual frustration.

'I thought not.' There was a definite chuckle in the elderly man's voice. 'When I phoned earlier to invite you both to dinner tomorrow evening I was told in no uncertain terms that the two of you were not, on any account, to be disturbed. He has taken you to his home, yes? He said so. He is, I think, very much in love with you. Sometimes it happens like that—a bolt of lightning, I believe. Though I have never experienced such a thing.'

He gave a tiny sigh—although Bonnie admitted she might have imagined it—then, 'Had I known his preferred home was only a few miles from mine I would have gone there myself and faced him. I knew I would never get past first base if I'd tried to meet him at his business premises. My son is good at building high walls around himself, keeping his whereabouts and doings from outsiders—especially from the gentlemen of the press and his business rivals. It is part of his great success. However, the gods know best, and I sent you to find him—'

'Andreas.' Bonnie butted in at full volume. She couldn't bear to listen to any more babbling on about Dimitri falling for her and the wisdom of the gods! 'All I'm interested in is how your meeting went.' Not badly by the sound of things. A dinner invitation wouldn't have been extended if Dimitri had refused to end his vendetta, refused to try to build bridges.

'It went better than I had any right to hope,' he enthused, and then, after a telling pause, 'Dimitri hasn't told you?'

'It's a private matter, so he says.'

'Ah. I think I understand.' He sounded troubled now. 'But there should be no secrets between husband and wife. Nothing of any magnitude kept back and hidden.'

An opinion Bonnie wholeheartedly agreed with. She let that confirmation pass and commented starchily, 'I am not going to be his wife. I can't think where you got *that* idea from.'

She earned herself a gentle chuckle. 'You sound exactly as you did on the one and only time I objected to your dietary restrictions.' And then, much more soberly, 'This won't be easy for me, but please listen to what I have to tell you.'

Twenty minutes later Bonnie was making rapid if stumbling progress back to the house, her heart full to bursting point with emotion.

If only he'd told her!

Why hadn't he told her?

Determined to face him with what she now knew, she increased her speed. She needed to calm down, cool off before she faced him. Red-faced and sweaty, her hair like a long tangled mop, a great rip in her dress where in her haste she'd caught it in a bush, she knew she looked a total wreck.

Just like her emotions.

Her head down, she skidded to a halt as a cool, clipped voice enquired frigidly, 'Where have you been?'

Dimitri!

Under her breath she uttered a word that would have had her mother heading for her at outraged speed with soap and water. Then Bonnie snapped her head back and met the cool censure of his eyes.

Her heart flipped over, then jumped up and lodged in her throat. As always, he looked sensational. Intensely male, mind-numbingly sexy, as calm and collected as if he'd been in a boardroom, not taking a two-hour hike under the hot Greek sun to work off his temper. The aristocratic blade of his nose was just a little pinched, though, and the sensual mouth was more compressed than usual. The fathomless depths of his eyes were a little darker, and definitely bleaker.

He was standing on the terrace a scant two feet away. And she was a hot, sweaty, out-of-control mess. Couldn't be helped.

'Why didn't you tell me?' she launched, before she lost her nerve. 'Why leave me to struggle with the concept of loving a man who was nasty-minded enough to set out to destroy his own father because of some slight received in childhood that any normal person would have forgiven and forgotten after a couple of months?'

His eyes fell to the mobile gripped in her hand. 'You have been speaking to my father.'

'And not before time,' Bonnie came back. He looked really, really grim. Any underling discovered in some small mistake would melt gratefully into the floorboards on receipt of such a look.

But not her!

She lifted her chin. 'It wasn't easy for him, but he told me what he'd done and how heavily it's been lying on his conscience. Your mother worked for him as a servant. He seduced her—his first marriage was tired, as he put it. Your mother became pregnant, with you, and he told her she had to leave and forgot all about her. Until you turned up. A gangly, poorly dressed fourteen-year-old, he described you, asking for financial help because she was ill. He refused and, as he learned later, she died not long after.'

She stepped closer. He'd been pale beneath his warm, olive-toned skin, but now colour slashed across his fabulous cheekbones. 'I can understand how you must have hated the man who refused to acknowledge you as his son, who refused to give just a little financial help when it had to be obvious it was needed.' Smoky eyes searched his. 'But I don't understand why you didn't tell me.'

'No?' He expelled a short, sharp sigh. Then a wry smile touched his mouth. 'No, perhaps you don't.' He took a step towards her, looped an arm around her waist. 'Come inside. It is cooler. You shouldn't go charging around like a bullock let out into a field for the first time—not in this heat.'

The distinctly unflattering comparison didn't provoke a snappy comeback. She was beyond that—way beyond. She simply couldn't understand why a man who said he wanted her as his wife, in the closest relationship two people could achieve, should allow her to go on thinking that his vendetta of many years was down to some mere falling-out, a slight difference of opinion, when it had been something so much deeper and darker.

Had she agreed to follow her heart instead of her head and married him, would they have gone through life together with her never knowing of the trauma he must have suffered? The trauma that had led him on the path of vengeance? Would he *never* have trusted her with the secret of what had driven him?

Almost listlessly, she allowed him to lead her back into the house. Passing through the kitchen, he paused to pour her a tall glass of water.

'Drink. You must learn not to go out in the afternoon sun at this time of year. Not without sunblock and a shady hat.'

His smile touched her on the raw. She took the glass, but refused his advice. 'I don't need lectures, Dimitri!'

'You may not need them, *pethi mou*, but I shall deliver them when I think they're needed.'

He wasn't taking her seriously! She could smack him! Stamping ahead of him into the long, cool sitting room, she slumped onto one of the sofas and had to lift the glass with two hands because they were shaking. She emptied it thirstily.

She needed to cool down—regain her composure. He was standing above her, hovering.

'I need to shower and change,' she said, looking up at him. She'd wear the stuff she'd travelled to Greece in, and as soon as she got home she'd cut this horrid dress into polishing rags—all it was fit for. 'And then I want you to drive me to the airport.'

She'd sounded decisive—she was sure she had. So why was he dropping down beside her, his far too handsome features softening with something odd? Tenderness? Surely not. She couldn't, *wouldn't* let herself think that.

'So you would run away from what you know we have?' It was a gentle enquiry that had the effect of raising her temperature to boiling point.

'Great sex, you mean? That's not enough for me. Call me greedy—and I know you're a Greek male and must have inbred chauvinistic tendencies a mile wide—but I'm not what you'd deem to be suitable marriage material! I won't be any man's biddable little wife, happy to do what the lord and master wants and, heaven forbid, never asking questions!' She spluttered, the splutter produced in reaction to the way he'd had the gall to take both her hands in his.

She should snatch her hands away, sit on them as she'd been driven to do before. But, as always, his touch weakened her to such an extent that her self-protective instincts disappeared in a puff of smoke, and the sheer impact of his smile made her heartbeats quicken alarmingly.

'Bonnie—listen to me.' His fingers tightened unforgivably around hers. 'I am not proud of what I did in pursuit of revenge for what happened all those years ago. And I want you to believe that just before I met you I'd decided that the dish of vengeance was tasting sour. The idea of channelling my energies in another direction entirely was suddenly appealing. And then I met you, fell in love with you within a matter of a week, and I knew without one shadow of doubt where that direction lay.'

All the colour ebbed from Bonnie's face. He'd actually said he loved her! Her lips parted, but no sound emerged as he lifted her hands to his lips, then raised his head, his eyes brilliant. 'I didn't answer your questions because I didn't want to. Try to understand. I'd already had a taste of being on shaky ground with you—the way I'd let you believe I was one of my own staff and not the man you were looking for. Knowing what I know now, it was unforgivable. I had two choices: to let you go on thinking I was the type of man to hold a grudge over something you would think relatively unimportant, or to tell you what had driven me down that path. I found I was unable to do that,' he acknowledged grimly.

'But why?' Bonnie cried.

For answer he slid an arm around her and pulled her close, so that her head was cradled against the solid strength of his shoulder. 'Because you'd nursed Andreas, become fond of him. And that great well of compassion you have made you pity him for his obvious regrets for the man he had been, his distress. I can see and understand why he didn't tell you the whole of it—how he'd refused to help Eleni, my mother, when she so badly needed it. Just the tiniest fraction of his vast wealth would have enabled her to take some ease, prolong her life—the life that was so precious to me. But you became his champion, giving up your free time to chase down his son with a message he wanted delivered.'

His arms tightened around her. 'Simple male that I am, Bonnie, after my meeting with my father, after his contrition made him weep, my heart softened. I forgave him. Absolutely. And, that being so, I saw him as part of our family. A grandfather to our children. I wiped that part of the past out, wanted only a future with you. I didn't want to tell you the truth of it and see your fondness for the old man turn into disgust for what he'd done.'

Not simple—just single-minded! Bonnie twisted in his arms, her eyes sparkling, holding his. 'You can be so stupid!' she accused, her soft mouth wobbling. 'I *knew* something was troubling Andreas. Something he was deeply sorry for—but if someone is truly contrite, and he was, *is*, then anything can be forgiven! Of course I wouldn't turn against him, split a family just after the two of you had become reconciled! What do you take me for?'

'The most beautiful, the most straightforward, the most generous-hearted woman I have ever had the good fortune to meet. The only thing missing—' he bent his dark head to taste her mouth '—is for you to tell me you love me half as much as I love you.'

'Oh!' Bonnie wound her arms around his neck, her heart almost bursting. 'I *do* love you, you stubborn, simple man! But—' she drew back her head, her smooth brows pulling together '—can you be absolutely, utterly and completely sure that you're not just asking me to marry you, because you think I might be pregnant and, unlike your father, you face your responsibilities?'

This earned her a huge grin, and a kiss that left her weak with longing. Her knees actually buckled as he drew her to her feet and murmured, 'Absolutely, utterly and completely. And if you want me to prove it I'd marry you tomorrow, could it be arranged! Now...' His voice held that husky, sexy note that made her feel she was about to expire from excitement. 'I think we both need a shower.'

Aflame with happiness, Bonnie allowed him to lead her upstairs, not letting go of her for a single moment.

Nor did she make any objection when he stripped

off her horrid dress before they reached the state-of-
the-art bathroom, and lovingly removed her under-
wear as soon as the door was closed behind them.

EPILOGUE

As THE two sturdy figures flew towards him, Dimitri felt his heart swell with pride and devotion. Wet from their frolics in the shallow paddling pool he'd constructed with his own hands, the twins, Andreas and Eleni, were second only in beauty to his beloved wife.

He caught them in his arms, oblivious to the soaking of his grey silk suit. They were dark-haired, as he was, but possessed their mother's huge smoky grey eyes, and he adored them.

Almost as much as he adored the woman walking more sedately towards him, her smile only for him—her beautiful smile. She was heavy with his coming child. His own smile enfolded her.

'So this is what Greek men do—keep their wives barefoot and pregnant! I love it!' She laughed, catching him noticing her bare feet.

He slid the twins down his impressive length and caught Bonnie's hands in his. Their eyes met and held. Black and grey, drowning in love. Nearly four years of marriage, and life couldn't be better.

'I've something to tell you.' He drew her into his arms, his lips nuzzling the fragrance of her lovely hair. 'Today I have become unemployed.'

Bonnie tipped her head, eyeing him suspiciously. Getting on for four years of marriage and he could still spring surprises. 'And?'

'I have made a stand.' He grinned, referring to the time she had stood her ground, when he'd suggested, not without a pang, that with two babies in their cradles and her stated desire to have more, they should move to a larger home, architect-built to their own specifications.

'Certainly not.' She'd been adamant. 'Just build an extension.' Which he had—almost twice as large as the original farmhouse. Large enough to house as many children as she wanted, plus—at his insistence—a live-in nanny. Not to mention Andreas, who sometimes stayed over for a couple of days, or her family, arriving sometimes *en masse* for a holiday.

He drew her to the table sited beneath the shade of a sprawling fig tree. 'Today I finalised the sale of all my business enterprises.' He sat, settled her on his knee, his hand gently on the swell of her tummy. 'At a vast profit, naturally.'

'Naturally!' Bonnie turned and nuzzled her face into his neck. She loved him so much. 'But won't you miss the cut and thrust?'

'No, my dearest love, I will not.' He dipped his dark head, found her lips, lingered. 'What I did miss was you, when I had no option but to attend business meetings abroad. I couldn't concentrate as I knew I should. I was in torment!'

'And we can't have that!' Bonnie breathed against his lips. She had never known such love could exist. Her heart was almost bursting with it when he smiled against her mouth.

'Naturally not. The great Dimitri Kyriakis, unable to concentrate on his latest deal? Unheard of. But I will have no problem concentrating on becoming the complete family man—the complete and devoted lover of my beautiful wife.'

And Bonnie had no argument with that.

millsandboon.co.uk Community

Join Us!

The Community is the perfect place to meet and chat to kindred spirits who love books and reading as much as you do, but it's also the place to:

- **Get the inside scoop from authors about their latest books**
- **Learn how to write a romance book with advice from our editors**
- **Help us to continue publishing the best in women's fiction**
- **Share your thoughts on the books we publish**
- **Befriend other users**

Forums: Interact with each other as well as authors, editors and a whole host of other users worldwide.

Blogs: Every registered community member has their own blog to tell the world what they're up to and what's on their mind.

Book Challenge: We're aiming to read 5,000 books and have joined forces with The Reading Agency in our inaugural Book Challenge.

Profile Page: Showcase yourself and keep a record of your recent community activity.

Social Networking: We've added buttons at the end of every post to share via digg, Facebook, Google, Yahoo, technorati and de.licio.us.

www.millsandboon.co.uk

SAVE OVER £60

Free L'Occitane Gift Set worth OVER £10

**As you enjoy reading Mills & Boon® Modern™
titles we are offering you the chance to
sign up for 12 months and SAVE £61.25 –
that's a fantastic 40% OFF.**

**If you prefer, you can sign up for 6 months and
SAVE £19.14 – that's still an impressive 25% OFF.**

When you sign up you will receive 4 BRAND-NEW Modern
titles a month priced at just £1.91 each if you opt for a 12-
month subscription or £2.39 each if you opt for 6 months.
The full price of each book would normally cost you £3.19.

*PLUS, to say thank you, we will send you a
FREE L'Occitane Gift Set worth over £10*.*

You will also receive many more great benefits, including:
- **FREE home delivery**
- **EXCLUSIVE Mills & Boon® Book Club™ offers**
- **FREE monthly newsletter**
- **Titles available before they're in the shops**

Subscribe securely online today and SAVE up to 40% @ www.millsandboon.co.uk

*Gift set has an RRP of £10.50 and includes Verbena Shower Gel 75ml and Soap 110g.

SUB_0909_P9ZEN